Darkest Day

Book Two of the What She Knew Trilogy

K. R. Hughes
T. L. Burns

Master Koda Select Publishing

Disclaimer

Working on this trilogy was both fun and educational, though it is purely fictional. We scoured the local library and internet for any and all resources from the time period and then together, we weaved our own theory about what could have happened on that dark day in 1963 and the ensuing months. As with all good fictional stories, we leave it to you, the reader, to determine how much could be true, but more importantly, to enjoy the what if . . .

This is a work of historical fiction. All names, characters, and incidents are used fictitiously.

Connect with us on our website at
www.whatsheknew.wixsite.com/kandtproductions

Preface

Recap: The **What She Knew** trilogy is a fast-paced story of intrigue and mystery involving America's favorite sex goddess, Marilyn Monroe, with a conspiracy twist. On the night of Marilyn's death, she is rescued, and a body double takes her place. While the world believes she's dead, Marilyn and her allies race to utilize 'what she knew' to save John F. Kennedy from assassination.

Fateful Night, book one in the **What She Knew** trilogy, opens in late July 1962, just before the night of Marilyn Monroe's 'suicide' and ends with President John F. Kennedy's motorcade on Nov 22, 1963 in Dealey Plaza.

Darkest Day, book two in the **What She Knew** trilogy, picks up where ***Fateful Night*** leaves off. Was 'what she knew' enough to save Kennedy from being assassinated? Who is behind the plot to kill the president? Are they gunning for America or is it of a more personal nature? Keep reading to discover more of what she knew.

With Special Thanks To

A special thank you goes out to our publisher, Kim Mutch Emerson, and our editor, Arlene O'Neal. Without the encouragement and help of these two amazing ladies this book wouldn't be what it is today. We appreciate your help, patience, and input during the final stages and editing of this novel. We not only respect the integrity of your work but love you as family. Literally, we could not have published this book without you both.

Chapter 1

November 22, 1963

Bobby finished his early morning run, springing lightly onto the porch as he had done so many times in the past. It started as any other day, calm and peaceful enough. Later there would be meetings and hearings as well as his brother's motorcade ride through Dallas.

Thank God, they got Oswald in custody before he could do any real damage. Bobby sighed, as Ethel came out on the porch and handed him a wet rag and cool glass of ice water.

"Did you have a nice run, honey?" she asked, taking the end of the rag and swishing it around his hand playfully.

Bobby nodded. *Yep, just another normal morning at home with my wife.*

"Uh huh, I'm going in to shower." Bobby kissed her on the forehead, turned to the screen door, and went inside. Ethel followed him with a good-natured pat on the butt as she closed the screen door behind her.

The phone rang as they entered the hallway, he picked up the receiver. "Hello," Bobby answered, listening for a second, before his eyes widened, "What the hell?"

Bobby slammed down the receiver. "I have to go to Dallas, they've released Oswald!"

Throwing her hand up to cover her heart, Ethel squeaked, "Oh dear Lord, why?"

"I didn't ask," Bobby told her as he raced toward the stairs.

"Will you make it in time?" Ethel started to follow him.

"Yes, call and get the jet! I have to get ready." Bobby ran upstairs leaving a startled Ethel behind.

As Bobby got close to the top of the stairs, he stopped and looked down at Ethel, "Call the White House and get an urgent message to O'Donnell to watch out for Oswald and warn John!"

Lee Harvey Oswald strolled casually down the alleys of Dallas, TX with a huge duffle bag strapped to his back. He had carefully packed it early that morning and was side stepping the crowded streets with ease taking the more secluded route to the rendezvous point. Months of planning and lying to Marina had finally gotten him to this place, the one place he had always wanted to be. In the center of the arena proving who he really was.

Now as he stepped into the nearly abandoned building, his heart pounding rapidly in his chest, he wondered if he could fulfill this mission. *I will kill the president; then Castro will know who is really a great soldier for his team. I will accomplish my dreams.*

The shadowy figure of a man stood in one corner behind a pile of wooden crates. Oswald walked closer but stopped when the man held out his hand.

"So, you do own some balls after all. I never would have believed it." Sam Giancana laughed, a short harsh sound, as Oswald ran a nervous hand over his forehead.

Oswald put his hand down and forced a more-manly posture, "My mission is and has always been to make certain that the people are liberated from a dual democracy. I will do whatever is needed to prove to Fidel Castro that I'm his right-hand man."

"Well, if you do your job today, you will have everything you've ever dreamed of." Giancana turned to leave the room, but added over his shoulder, "The best vantage point is on the sixth floor, but you already know that."

Oswald swallowed hard, "Yes, and I won't let you down. My loyalty to Fidel is unfailing."

"We'll see." Giancana disappeared.

Yes, you will. Oswald laughed under his breath as he began climbing the stairs. *Then I'll have your respect as well as Castro's.*

Marilyn sat at the kitchen table reading the newspaper and sipping a cup of coffee as Ethel rushed into the room making disgusted noises. Marilyn watched her as she searched quickly in the cabinet, found what she wanted, and sloshed hot coffee into a metal mug.

As Ethel jerked open another cabinet door, the hinge came loose as the door nearly smacked her in the head.

"Ethel, slow down. What's the matter?" Marilyn asked as she laid the paper down beside her.

"That lunatic, Oswald, has been released and Bobby is rushing to get on the jet," Ethel had turned to Marilyn with the steaming cup still in her hand, "I just thought I'd fix him a cup of coffee and some muffins for the road."

"What?" Marilyn jumped up from her chair, toppling it to the floor with a loud clanking noise.

"Bobby got a call a few minutes ago. O'Donnell has been alerted and hopefully the secret service knows by now. I called to let them know."

"My God, I knew this would happen. I'm going with him!" Marilyn scrambled up from the table, leaving her dishes behind as she raced from the room.

Across the globe in Greece as Aristotle Onassis slept, he muttered, "A Kennedy free world. Die Mr. President, die."

He would know in a few short hours whether the plan had been followed or not. Ari snorted a laugh in his sleep, startling the woman in the bed next to him. Ari tossed his arms wide, "I'm free and now you're my puppet."

She got out of bed, found her skimpy clothing, and tip toed to the door. As she was quietly opening it, she heard a dreaming Aristotle mutter, "I've got you now, you bastard, and soon, I'll have that scum brother of yours too." This eerie proclamation was followed by a victorious evil laugh which caused the young woman to flee.

Chapter 2

Bobby and Marilyn were in the air on a hurried flight to Dallas, TX. Marilyn was putting on her make-up while Bobby stared moodily out the window. Marilyn looked over the travel mirror, and froze her hand with the mascara wand in mid-air to watch him for a moment.

"We'll get there in time. It'll be okay. It just has to be." Marilyn tried to reassure him as she finished applying the black to her lashes. She placed the brush back in the tube and screwed the lid on while balancing the mirror with the ease of long habit.

"How can you even worry about make-up at a time like this?" Bobby shook his head, a little snicker escaping from his lips. "I know, I know," he held up a hand to stop her protest,

"Ethel tells me all the time a woman wouldn't be caught dead without her make-up."

"It's true, but it is also such a mundane task. It forces normalcy into the equation and helps me think clearer."

Marilyn had taken out the blush and was now applying it to each cheek. Bobby shook his head again and sighed.

"Well, at any rate it gives you something to occupy your hands." Bobby stared out the window for a second. "When we land there will be a car ready to take us straight to the motorcade. I hope that we will have some new information as soon as we get there."

"Me too," She checked her face in the mirror for a second, "What do you want me to do?" Marilyn had replaced the blush in the make-up case and zipped it closed. She put it on the table at her elbow and picked up the comb.

"I think you should just mingle in the crowds and watch for anyone who looks out of place. I don't think he'll have time to get anywhere near Dealy Plaza with the blockades and cops but I can't risk it."

"Whatever you need me to do, I'm there for you and for Jack." Marilyn finished styling her hair and got out the can of hairspray.

Bobby held up his hand, "No way, you're spraying that in here! I won't be able to breathe for hours."

"We're going to Texas, right? The wind is awful there. You don't want me to have hair in my face while I'm trying to save Jack, do you?"

"Take it to the bathroom. I can't stand that junk." Bobby made a face.

Marilyn laughed, picked up her hairspray and walked the short distance to the bathroom.

6

Bobby called to her, "And shut the door! The fumes will still get in here. Use the fan."

"Oh for Pete's sake you're such a girl sometimes. No, I take that back, any girl worth her eye shadow inhales fumes of all kinds for the greater good." Marilyn laughed through the closed door. "What we women do to have a beautiful face is nearly as insane as Oswald."

Bobby sat starring out the window, watching the fluffy clouds drift by underneath the wings of the plane. *How anyone could have considered her a dumb blonde is beyond me.* Bobby picked up the cigarette case at his elbow, pulled one out and lit it up.

Inhaling a calming drag of nicotine, he sat back in his chair. *Latimer and Stansel will be at the scene with the other secret service men. But can I trust the others? Doubtful. Man, what a mess! The real question is; can we get to them all in time? Has the president been warned and did Kenny put everyone on high alert?*

Bobby gave himself a mental shake, *Of course he did. Now think like that madman Oswald.*

Marilyn returned from the bathroom and sat down just as the pilot announced five minutes to landing.

Agent Latimer rushed toward Bobby standing on a downtown street in Dallas, TX awaiting the motorcade of the president.

"Mr. Kennedy. We've got both Oswald and Bannister in custody. Security is beefed up and we're trying to persuade the limo driver to put the top up."

"Good work, Latimer. I think we should be safe enough now. If we can get through this next hour, we'll be in the clear...well until next time." Bobby shifted his feet nervously.

"We won't fail you, Mr. Kennedy. Stansel and I will both be walking alongside the motorcade."

"Thanks, Latimer."

Bobby paced the walk waiting for the president to make his appearance. *Onassis, you Greek bastard, I'm onto you.*

The president helped the first lady into the limo. He patted her hand and climbed in beside her. Just as the car began to roll he spotted someone on the sidewalk. *No, it can't be.*

He did a double take as the car rounded the first corner and he could see the face clearly in the sunlight. *It's not, it can't be. Marilyn?*

As the car moved out of view she lifted her hand to her lips and blew her famous kiss his way.

Stansel was out of breath when he reached Latimer. "We don't have him!"

"What do you mean, 'we don't have him'?" Latimer's eyes were nearly popping out of his head. "What happened, the CIA said they had Oswald and Bannister?"

"They do have Bannister, but the other man is not Oswald."

Lyndon Johnson, with his wife Lady Bird, sat in the open car, a secret service vehicle traveling in between them and the Kennedy's open limo, several car lengths ahead of the vice president and guests, the Yarboroughs.

Johnson was seething at the warm reception that had greeted the president and his beautiful young wife. Johnson was also upset that his enemy Yarborough was seated in the car with him while the presidential couple were with his long-time friends the Connelly's.

The crowds covered the sidewalks on both sides of the street and were loudly cheering and chanting the president's name. They were also screaming about Jackie's beauty and elegance. The Kennedy's were receiving these accolades with a gracious nod or wave to the crowd.

"Turn on the news coverage of this motorcade." Johnson yelled to the driver. "Make sure it's loud."

The driver glanced in the rearview mirror looking at Johnson, *What an odd request.* He turned on the radio without comment.

"I said turn it on LOUD. I want to drown out this noisy crowd." Johnson bellowed at the driver.

Suddenly the volume was cranked up and the announcer on the radio crackled, "The president and Mrs. Kennedy have been greeted to enthusiastic cheers by a seemingly endless crowd. The president's car is stopping so that he can shake hands with some of the spectators."

Johnson seemed unmoved but continued to scowl as his car crept slowly along the route in order to give the president's vehicle a wide berth.

Lady Bird shifted in the seat, she was overly warm since the top was down on the car. The air was humid and sticky making the ride uncomfortable.

Marilyn finished her wave and covered her hair with a scarf. She turned to make her way through the crowd, and frowned as she made it to a store front to the back of the spectators who were hanging off the sidewalk and trying to follow the presidential vehicle on foot. *Something just doesn't seem quite right.*

Lee Harvey Oswald stood carefully aiming the gun behind the boxes of books in the depository. His aim was accurate and his confidence began to soar as his anger grew. *I'll get him with just one shot and he'll be dead.*

He watched with hatred as the first car passed by. He scanned the third of the open cars, and watched as all of the stupid passengers' waved at the crowd, with the exception of Johnson who looked sullen. Through the scope of the gun, he swung back to the president's car.

Kennedy was relaxed and happy as the procession inched along. Oswald shifted his scope a quarter of an inch then back to its original place. *Steady now, soon the president will be approaching. Calm yourself and focus on this task. Fidel Castro will know that I'm a trustworthy soldier in just a couple more minutes. Then true victory will be mine.* He inhaled a deep breath and let it out with a great burst of air hissing through his teeth.

Oswald shifted on the balls of his feet to glance out the window. The president was closest to him; the shot would be clean. *Perfect.* Not only that, but the car was moving slower than expected which would make getting a clean round off even easier.

Crouching behind the gun, Oswald took careful aim as he watched the car inch closer with his finger poised on the trigger.

Bobby stood close to the area where Marilyn was waiting for him. He could just see her standing against the window of the shop across the street. She was looking around with a confused gaze.

Suddenly, she saw him, she smiled, and waved. He gave a short wave back then made his way through the crowd, across the street, and was just stepping onto the sidewalk next to her when a sudden 'pop' filled the air. Then two more; just like firecrackers in celebration.

Startled, the crowd buzzed with questions as Marilyn registered the sound and her face showed the panic seizing her.

"Oh my Lord, a shot has just been fired. The president has been shot. It appears that the president has been shot." The panicked announcer nearly screamed into the microphone blaring through the speakers of the vice president's vehicle.

Chapter 3

The house was quiet when a noise awakened Robert Allen at nine in the morning. His room was darkened by black out blinds which allowed him to sleep after his long nights of partying.

He stirred and tried to go back to sleep but the hairs on the back of his neck stood up as he realized there was movement just inside the room.

His sleep filled eyes slowly adjusted to the figures silently coming toward him in the darkness. He barely made out the two men as he saw one of them swoop down at him with a knife in his hand. He rolled, just out of the grasp of a masked man in what appeared to be a dark suit.

As he landed on the floor off the other side of the bed, he jumped up, and took one step into a hulking man who grabbed his arms, jerking them behind his back while his assistant placed a gag in Robert's mouth.

Too stunned to even fight back Robert just stood there while a cloth was placed over his nose and mouth. Wrenching back at the acrid smell of the chloroform he struggled but ended in a heap on the floor in a dead faint.

"Modern science is great. I love these knock out drops." The huge man placed a lit flashlight on top of the skewed blankets on the bed. He picked Robert up like he was a rag doll and flung him into a chair.

The other man, slight in build, was busy digging in the closet; he flung clothing off the rod and then raked the contents of the lone shelf onto the floor. Sweeping the mess with a flashlight, the slighter man reached for the light switch.

The big man blinked for a moment as the light blared dispersing the darkness. He continued to securely tie Robert Allen to the chair; hands, feet, and around the mid-section. "Did you find them?"

"Not yet. I didn't think they'd be in plain sight." The slight guy lifted the wool mask from his face for a moment to wipe away the sweat. "God, how does he sleep in this heat?"

"He's not cultured, my friend."

"Yes, he's obviously not a Yale or Harvard man." The smaller man straightened his tie and began dumping the contents of the dresser into the middle of the floor.

"We'll just have to ask him where they are when he wakes up. I doubt it will be a pleasant conversation."

Clint Hill leapt from the secret service car in front of the presidential vehicle and ran toward the president's slumped form. He watched in horror as Jacqueline Kennedy hovered over the trunk of the car pulling in what appeared to be pieces of skull and hair off the dark metal.

Reaching the Kennedy limo, Hill jumped onto the back of the car and pushed Jackie in, shielding her in the event of further bullets.

Oswald stepped calmly away from the window. He pushed the gun behind the boxes and whistled happily as he strolled out of the room, down the hall and out into the mayhem he had just created, leaving behind his gun and jacket in his euphoria.

People came running out of rooms where they had been leaning in windows watching the procession of the president and first lady. They were running around in terror screaming.

One lady rushed at him, grabbed his arm. Her face was panicked as she cried out, "Did you hear? The president's been shot."

Oswald shook himself free of her hysterics and moved on down the stairs without a word or backward glance.

Bobby stood motionless for a single second while he tried to piece together what had just occurred. Agent Latimer leapt to his side and led him away from the street into the privacy of a now empty store.

Bobby shook himself back to reality and demanded, "What just happened?"

"The president has been shot."

"I need to go to him." Bobby, frantic, started toward the glass door but Latimer stood in front of it. "My God, let me through." Bobby growled through gritted teeth.

"My job is to protect you, sir." Latimer crossed his arms over his chest and planted his feet.

"Like you protected the president? No thanks." Bobby pushed at Latimer and tried to get past him.

"Sir, I really don't want to use force to keep you from getting shot as well, but I will." Latimer refused to budge as they stared each other down.

"I need a phone!" Bobby turned and ran toward the back of the store, searching for an office.

Latimer could be heard on his radio, "I've got him, come on in Stansel."

Aristotle Onassis answered the phone on the first ring. "Yes?" he said hopefully.

"The president of the United States has been shot." The answer came from a pip-squeaky voice that sounded more like a teenage boy than a real man.

"That is excellent news, most excellent indeed." Aristotle laughed into the phone, "You have made my day." Ari glanced at the clock hanging up the receiver as he muttered, "It's close enough to high noon for it to work."

Marilyn found a pay phone, slipped inside the box and picked up the receiver pressing 'O' for the operator.

"Operator, how can I assist you?"

"I need to place a person to person call to Ethel Kennedy."

"Hold the line please."

The operator came back on the line a few seconds later, "All lines are busy. Please hang up and try again."

"That's bull shit!" Marilyn clanged the receiver into its cradle, stomped her foot, and moved out of the booth as she looked around for a solution. *Shit. Now what to do?*

McGeorge Bundy, director for national security, sat in his office catching up on piles of paperwork. It was quiet at the White House since everything was going on in Dallas. The offices had been redone while the president had been chasing about the globe. The workers had finally finished with the racket and peace reigned for the moment at least.

His phone rang breaking the silence, startling him, he spoke gruffly.

"Bundy."

"This conversation never happened," barked an audibly upset Bobby, "I need you to take care of the president's personal files ASAP."

Without hesitation, "Yes, sir, consider it done."

"I think you should know the president has been shot. Has word reached there yet?"

"No."

"Good. Keep it to yourself for now. No word yet on his condition. I'll check back with you in an hour." Bobby hung up.

McGeorge Bundy sat for a moment in stunned silence, shook his head sadly, then got up to do Bobby's bidding.

Bundy stumbled down the hall in a fog. Saddened and numb. Mechanically he changed the locks on JFK's private files. Mentally checking it off his list he found a security guard.

"Come with me, you have a top secret job to do." Bundy commanded.

"But sir, I'm to guard this door."

"Nothing is more important than this. Come with me now."

He had the more sensitive documents moved to the Executive Office Bldg., where he placed the guard there. "Someone must guard these things around the clock until further notice. I'll send someone to relieve you in several hours.

Make sure no one touches them or knows where they came from."

The guard nodded at his orders and took a protective stance near the cabinet.

Bundy left to take care of the oval office and cabinet room. He ordered them debugged from his favored secret service men who came in wearing pest control uniforms.

Having completed the requests, Bundy sighed heavily and headed back to his office. The phone rang as he was sitting down at his desk.

"Hello."

"Our fears have been confirmed. The president is dead." Clint hung up without waiting for a reply.

Chapter 4

Frank Sinatra, Ava and Zsa-Zsa Gabor, Bob Mitchum, Bing Crosby, Shirley McClain, and Doris Day all sat around the comfortable lodge in Cal-Neva with "As the World Turns" on low in the background. Everyone had just finished breakfast as they relaxed in the main room, just laughing and talking.

Suddenly the broadcast was interrupted by Walter Cronkite, "In Dallas, Texas, three shots were fired at President Kennedy's motorcade in downtown Dallas. The first reports say that President Kennedy has been seriously wounded by this shooting."

All heads turned toward the TV where the face of Walter Cronkite, stricken and pale, appeared. The news broadcast immediately switched to camera shots of the Trade Mart in

Dallas where President Kennedy was to attend a luncheon. Frank sprang to the television to turn the volume up higher as everyone else sat in shocked silence.

As they all watched the television in disbelief, the camera panned across the Trade Mart ballroom to a black waiter who wiped tears from his eyes. The workmen are seen removing the Presidential seal from the podium where President Kennedy was to make his speech. Eddie Barker, a news affiliate in Dallas situated in Trade Mart for the upcoming luncheon, repeated the rumor over the microphone "that the president is dead." Walter Cronkite adds, "This is not confirmed but is the word we're getting. The President is dead."

Mrs. Connelly and Jacqueline stood around awaiting the news. Dottie Connelly had been forced to wait with the presidential party in a secured room. Her husband was downstairs in the Emergency Room with a gunshot wound to his back that had gone out through his chest.

"He's dead. I know he's dead." Jackie kept saying over and over.

"It'll be all right." Mrs. Connelly rallied beside a very bloody Jackie.

Finally, a sympathetic orderly took pity on the women and brought them some straight backed chairs and coffee.

As the secret service men surrounded Johnson in a hospital room, the women were left outside in the hallway. They had closed off the room then guarded Johnson with the rabid ferocity of a bull dog with a ham bone.

Jacqueline noted with insight, "There is only one reason they would guard the vice president like that. Jack's dead. I know he's dead. Why won't they just come out and tell us he's dead and end this nightmare?"

The sun was shining in the windows of the Brentwood home where Robert Allen sat, exhausted on a chair, still tied to the arms. His legs were hurting and numb, his throat parched and sore while his bladder was ready to explode. The men in ski masks and suits were still combing through his home with the ferocity seen in a championship football game's last minute.

The smaller man came in, still wearing his suit jacket and tie with the ridiculous ski mask covering his face. He looked over at Robert, noting the misery, "Are you ready to tell us where they are now?"

"No."

"So far, I've been very patient with you and this little game you've decided to play."

Robert tried to shift in his chair but couldn't move, "It is possible that if you had asked nicely I would have simply given you what you want."

The suited man laughed; a hard and ugly sound emitting from deep in his throat, "We both know that's not the truth. Now IF you give me those tapes I'll let you go without beating you senseless. I don't like to have bruised knuckles."

Robert gave a tight lipped chuckle, "I can't simply give them to you. They were put into my safe keeping and I intend to go down fighting."

"It's hardly a fight when you can't defend yourself. But have it your way." The man left the room and returned a moment later with the huge man.

Robert starred hard as they approached him, "So now you've brought Goliath to fight your battles. Some David you turned out to be."

The punch landed squarely on Robert's jaw and his head snapped with the impact. Had Goliath been a prize fighter he would have won with a TKO but he simply threw a glass of cold water in Robert's face.

Robert sputtered and spit out the blood pooling in his mouth as he regained consciousness. He opened his eyes and stared up at his attacker.

Wiggling his jaw, Robert spat again, "That must make you feel like a big man, Goliath, to hit someone who can't defend himself. Let's say you untie me and make this a fair fight."

"Let's say I don't." Goliath slapped him upside the left side of his head, leaving Robert's ear bright red. Then he punched him in the nose, which immediately drew blood. After that punch, Goliath smacked him with such force that the chair toppled over backward.

As the big man went to stand the chair back on its feet he noted that again his victim was out cold. "Weak little fucker isn't he?"

"Now you know I don't like that kind of language. We're educated men who don't need to speak crudely to be tough." The smaller man burst into growling laughter as Goliath smacked Robert's face to wake him.

"Had enough?"

"No, you'll have to do your worst. I am accountable to a true monster and he is far more menacing than you. Find what you're looking for, if you can, and get out of my house." Robert spat again and the crimson landed on his orange shag carpeting blending in nicely.

"I could kill you."

"It's preferable to giving them up. Do your worst. I'm ready to die."

Oswald walked up to the bus stop after leaving his house tucking his pistol in the pocket of his jacket. He looked nervously around him as he walked, checking over his shoulder and nearly stepping off the sidewalk in his fear.

They're following me. Late, late, late! Why did I leave that sorry ass blue jacket at work? This one has to be close enough. Please give me the code word so I can be safe.

Behind him he saw no one, but he knew *they* were there, watching him. He paused at the bus stop for a moment but he was too nervous to wait. He continued walking for another mile or so and slowed down.

A police car was following him. *What to do now? Act cocky? Casual? Maybe he'll pass on by.*

But the car pulled up beside him and the passenger window came down. "Sir, a word with you," called the officer inside the vehicle.

Oswald walked over to the squad car and leaned in a little but kept his face fully out of view of the cop.

"How can I help you officer?" Oswald's voice cracked. It sounded nervous even to his own ears.

"Just wondering why you're out roaming the street when everyone else is glued to the set watching the news of the president's shooting." Tibbet told him.

"I hadn't heard." Oswald lied.

Tibbet, sensing that something was amiss, cocked his head, "Can you step back over to the curb?"

"Is something wrong officer?" Oswald stepped back but seemed about to bolt.

Officer Tibbet stepped out of the car, leaving the door open and hurried around the front of the car.

As the officer came around toward the front, a blur of two men raced from behind the car. Tibbet stopped walking as they ran up to Oswald. One of the two men grabbed Oswald's gun.

"Hold it right there." Tibbet yelled reaching toward his holster for his own weapon. "This man matches the description of the assassin."

"I'm here to assist you officer," Jimmy Fratianno smiled, held the gun steady and shot the officer four times.

Tibbet fell into the street, dead.

"Here," Fratianno thrust the gun back into Oswald's hand. "Run."

"Where are they? I'm late to the rendezvous place and I don't have the right color jacket." Oswald panicked as he pointed the gun at Giancana and Fratianno.

"Steady there, you lousy son of a bitch. If you shoot us you won't get away, now will you? I knew you didn't have balls." Giancana leered.

Oswald tucked the gun in his jacket but stood rooted to the sidewalk.

"Run, they're waiting about a half mile west of here." Giancana shoved him hard in the right direction.

Oswald finally sprouted wings and ran away from the scene of the crime.

"Dumb bastard." Fratianno muttered, stepping over the deceased policeman. He leaned in the squad car, picked up the radio and waited for the operator to answer the call.

"I would like to report a downed officer." Fratianno calmly told her the location.

"Who are you sir?" the operator asked over the radio, "sir?"

But they had disappeared.

Frank and Ava sat quietly while everyone else began talking in horrified whispers. Frank leaned closer to the TV set hoping to hear more. As Walter Cronkite's face came back on the screen,

Frank turned to his friends and they all hushed in anticipation of the next update.

The camera panned to the newsroom clock, the time was exactly 2:37 P.M. CBS news editor Ed Bliss, Jr. handed Cronkite an AP wire report. Cronkite took a long second to read it to himself before addressing a shocked nation.

Ava sighed, a long and heavy hearted sound, muttering, "Tell us." She started to cry as Shirley leaned over and hugged the now sobbing Ava. Frank noted, *Tragedy can make friends of enemies, even if only for a moment.* As Frank mused, his thoughts were interrupted by a very sad Walter Cronkite.

"From Dallas, Texas, the flash, apparently official. President Kennedy died at 1:00 P.M. Central Standard Time, two o'clock Eastern Standard Time." He paused and looked at the studio clock. "Some thirty-eight minutes ago."

Momentarily losing his composure, Cronkite winced, removed his eyeglasses, and cleared his throat before he continued, "Vice President Lyndon Johnson will presumably take the oath of office to become the thirty-sixth president of the United States."

Chapter 5

Bobby sat numb, listless.

Latimer opened the door to the office, "Mr. Kennedy. I need to move you to a more secure location."

"What? Where? I need to be at the hospital with the president and first lady."

"Sorry, but that's not where we're going."

"I'm going to the hospital. My family needs me right now." Bobby stood up, "either I go with you or find my own way."

"Hold on, let me see what I can arrange." Latimer closed the door.

Bobby picked up the phone, dialed. After a few rings, Bundy answered.

"Status?"

"Taken care of."

"Good. Get me Walton. Have the call routed to this number."

"Yes, sir."

"Bundy, this is a matter of national security; I don't need to remind you to keep this under wraps."

"No, sir. Just to be clear sir, you mean Bill Walton, the Soviet liaison."

"That's correct."

Jack Ruby stood behind his bar, cleaning the inside of a glass with a rag. He was listening without much surprise to the news of the president's shooting.

Sam Giancana suddenly appeared at the end of the bar. "The bastard got away. He's getting on the bus down the street. Take care of him."

Jack Ruby tossed down the rag, put the glass on the counter top and ran out of the bar to chase the bus.

"Stupid patriotic bastard, he'll never get what he's bargained for either." Giancana helped himself to a stiff one and sat down at the bar.

Marilyn stood on the corner watching for a cab. "Damn it!"

Everything was utter chaos in the streets of Dallas. People were running around and yelling about the tragedy while the entire system of lights and electricity seemed to have failed at once.

"First the call to Ethel is cut off, and now this." Marilyn ground her teeth in frustration as she turned toward the bus stop, nearly colliding with the only other person on the street who seemed to be in his right mind. A very thin, worn looking man in a light grey jacket passed her heading for the same bus stop.

They arrived together and stood for a moment in silence, looking down the street for the bus.

"Morning," he surveyed her, though he looked agitated and pale.

"It's hardly a good morning. I do hope the president will live." Marilyn answered, clearly distracted. But he persisted.

"Lee."

"Norma."

The bus pulled up, Marilyn realized it wasn't hers but glanced at him as he got on. A man ran up suddenly, and jumped on the bus just as the driver was closing the door.

"Bastard, didn't you see me waving to wait?" The man hollered as the door closed and the bus pulled away.

Roselli picked up the receiver in the phone booth; he dialed a long number and waited impatiently for it to ring. After about thirty seconds the clicking, sporadic buzzing stopped and the connection was made.

"Yes?" came the sharp answer on the other end.

"I need to talk to Castro, NOW." Roselli barked at the assistant.

"Hang on Roselli, I'll get the senor."

Castro came on the line after a brief moment, "What's the problem now?"

"Oswald is free. But Giancana is taking care of him."

"Get that whinny bastard. We can't let him get arrested, he'll talk." Castro roared.

"We've got it covered." Roselli shot back.

"You better hope to Hell that you do." Castro slammed down the receiver.

Bill Walton jumped out of a Soviet cab and walked quickly into the restaurant, the Sovietskaya. It had been a long day burdened with the news of his message from the United States, but the urgency took precedence over his own exhausted needs.

Georgi Bolshakov, soviet agent for the U.S., sat at a table in a dark corner awaiting the rendezvous with Walton.

As Walton entered the restaurant, Bolshakov signaled to the waiter for more Vodka holding up two fingers. Walton joined him at the table a moment later while the waiter put down a glass for him and filled it. After the waiter had disappeared from ear shot, Walton delivered the first part of his message.

"Mr. Robert Kennedy wants you to know that the president is dead. He insisted I inform you in person so that you could tell the Soviet premier. Mr. Kennedy will continue to uphold the negotiations that have gone forward." Walton downed his Vodka in one gulp and signaled for another.

Bolshakov sat for several moments digesting what he had been told. Silence laid heavy about them.

"Please convey my deepest condolences to Robert. He well knows how much I admired his brother even while we had our differences." Bolshakov downed his Vodka, picked up the bottle the waiter had left and refilled both of their glasses.

"I will be happy too. It is imperative that Premier Khrushchev get this message tonight."

"Understood."

"Mr. Kennedy would also like to remind you of that last conversation you had at the White House 'In a gust of flying hate, his enemies may go to any length, including killing him.' It has cost the president of the United States his life to meet your premier half way. Do not let his death be in vain. We will make sure that your country still gets its missiles and we trust you will make sure your Premier holds up his end of our bargain."

Walton got up from the table and left a morose Bolshakov pondering in sadness the loss of the president and what it would mean for his beloved country, the former Russia.

Chapter 6

Marilyn had arrived at the newly opened Love Field airport hot, tired, and furious. Bobby was nowhere to be seen and the pilot refused to let her back on the plane. Marilyn took a seat in the private lounge where she ordered a stiff drink and sat just as stiff awaiting the attorney general.

On the television behind the bar, NBC's Frank McGee announced, "That this afternoon, wherever you were and whatever you might have been doing when you received the word of the death of President Kennedy, that is a moment that will be emblazoned in your memory and you will never forget it...as long as you live."

Marilyn threw back her drink and held her glass up for another. The bartender nodded his understanding and filled the glass with rum and coke. Marilyn dried her wet eyes with her handkerchief and sniffed into it.

As Bobby rushed for the plane, he never even stopped to see if Marilyn was in the lounge or on board his private jet. The pilot noticed that Bobby was running; rushed over to Marilyn and grabbed her.

"Come on, we have to go." He took hold of her arm and yanked her out of the seat, startling Marilyn enough to drop her drink and her composure.

Yelping, Marilyn started to protest but he pointed to Bobby's retreating back. "He'll have both of our heads. Hurry!"

"There will no doubt be heads rolling, but it won't be mine." Marilyn struggled to keep up with the pilot in her high heeled shoes.

Bobby was standing on the steps to the jet as they rushed up to meet him. He looked startled to see her then grew sheepish as he realized that Marilyn had been ditched in downtown Dallas.

"It wasn't my fault. I swear I had no choice." Bobby defended as Marilyn swept past him onto the plane.

Just what I need right now. The silent treatment. Bobby followed her on board and took his seat.

Jack Ruby had followed Oswald onto the bus. Oswald watched him yell at the driver and slunk toward the rear doors. As Ruby sat near the front, Oswald kicked the back door open and jumped off the bus; he rolled once, picked himself up and ran. The passengers were screaming as chaos broke out, the driver pulled the bus over to try and handle the crisis.

As the bus slowed, Ruby jumped from the front end and took off in pursuit of the assassin. "Come back here you bastard! I know what you did."

Seconds later Ruby rounded the corner in time to hear a shop owner from next door tell the manager of the movie theater that a man had snuck in without paying for a ticket in the back entrance.

"FBI," Ruby told the manager, "I'll go get him. He's wanted for questioning at HQ."

"What for?"

"Nothing major. Misdemeanor crime."

"Ok, thanks." The manager returned to making popcorn and opening bottles of soda for his demanding customers. Apparently, all were oblivious to the fact that the Leader of the Free world had just been shot.

Now as Ruby entered the movie theater looking for Oswald, he found him easily enough. The crazed man was wiping sweat from his forehead.

As Ruby got closer he silently snickered at his own cleverness. Oswald would be strangled and no one would ever know who did it. *I'll kill that crummy bastard just as this cancer is killing my body. I can rest in peace knowing that even though I couldn't save the president, I could at least make it harder for my true enemies to prosper. Finally, my family will be taken care of as they deserve and I get to serve justice to America in the name of my fallen president. True, I'll look like a crazed lunatic but I know the truth as do my comrades.* Ruby removed a length of rope from his pocket and wrapped it tightly around each hand twice.

As he was nearing the seat behind Oswald the house lights suddenly came up and cops surrounded the exits. Ruby sat down abruptly, tucking the rope back in his pocket as the cops neared where he was seated.

"Everyone stay where you are. Nobody move."

The theater was dead silent as the cops looked for their criminal. Terrified movie goers stared at each other as the policemen walked past each row guns in front of them scouring the crowd. They found him quick and grabbed him by his shirt collar, jerking him out of his seat.

The cops took a screaming Oswald into custody, cuffing him and dragging him out as the silence erupted into a loud buzz from the stunned crowd.

Oswald was hollering, "Police brutality, I didn't do anything. Police brutality. Somebody help me."

Jack Ruby slumped into the seat, hands covering his face and nearly cried at his failure, "Shit."

President Johnson, newly sworn in, sat quietly, trying to take in the sudden change in his status, with Lady Bird at his side. Lady Bird sat rehashing the feeble attempts she and Lyndon had made in order to comfort Jackie when she first arrived aboard Air Force One.

Soon it became evident that she could not be comforted; unfortunately, decorum was one of Lady Bird's favorite things.

"You may want to freshen up before the media gets a good look at you." Lady Bird had tweeted.

"I want them to see what they have done to Jack." Jacqueline was so furious; she had almost spat the words at her.

"I just thought you might want to freshen up before Lyndon takes the oath of office." Lady Bird had held her ground.

Jacqueline had just ignored her and stood with Johnson covered in the blood stains and brain matter from her husband's scalp.

Well, Lady Bird mused, *at a time like this, all ill manners must be excused. I just so wish this had not happened in my beloved state of Texas.*

Chapter 7

Giancana stood outside of Jack Ruby's bar impatiently awaiting his return. The news had already leaked that Oswald had been arrested and held for questioning in the assassination of the president.

"What a fucking nightmare." Sam kicked the door in. In his rage, he stomped into the bar, threw the first chair he came to through the front window and generally wrecked the place. On the chalkboard behind the bar he wrote two words. "Get him."

At the rear of the plane, Jacqueline Kennedy leaned over the casket stroking it with long, sad caresses.

The entire Kennedy camp was reeling from the last couple of hours and had retreated with her to the rear of the plane.

They were totally sectioning themselves away from the Johnson camp; after all, they were still considered the enemy.

Kenny O'Donnell, saddened and angry, tried to provide comfort to Jackie but there wasn't anything he could do. He was grieving every bit as much for his lost friend as the first lady was grieving for her husband perhaps more.

Johnson signaled for Kenny to come sit with him. Kenny patted Jacqueline's hand and rose to join the new president.

"Mr. O'Donnell I'd like for you to continue in the role you've always played for your president." Johnson seemed unsure, lost even; a foreign concept for a cocksure man.

"No thank you. My loyalties are with the Kennedy's. No disrespect intended but your politics are not something that I support."

"I realize that the Constitution of the United States is putting me into the White House," Johnson continued, "and there's not a law to make you stay there with me."

O'Donnell's face showed his contempt.

Johnson continued, pleading, "It is imperative that as one of the closest advisors to Kennedy, you should stay and stand shoulder to shoulder with me. The country needs you by my side."

Not wanting to create a scene, O'Donnell shook his head and muttered "I'll give it some thought."

Robert Kennedy stood beside his pilot anxiously as they flew back to the D.C. area. "Are we going to get to Andrews before Air Force One?"

"Yes, sir, I'll make certain that you are there to meet it." The pilot adjusted the throttle of the plane.

"Just get me there. Find out where it's touching down and be sure I'm the first one on it."

"I'll make radio connection with the tower, sir." The pilot picked up the handset as Robert Kennedy sat down in the co-pilot's seat.

Ethel sat nervously on the couch at home. "Pat, have you heard?" she asked into the receiver, "Jack has been assassinated."

"Yes, we've heard," Pat managed, barely maintaining her composure. "Peter is getting a few things together and we're headed out the door. Where are we meeting?"

"Bethesda Naval Hospital. God, can you even imagine? I feel so bad for poor Jackie." Ethel swung her foot nervously and wrapped her toes in the phone cord. "Sitting beside your husband as he is shot like that, right there in the car.

"Yes, me too, I mean even though we're not close it has to be horrible for her," Pat agreed, "However, he was my brother first and always." Pat sobbed for a moment but regained her composure quickly, as befitting a true Kennedy.

"I know how you must feel. What in the world possessed Jackie to climb onto the trunk of the car? I would have ducked for cover. Isn't that the natural instinct? Protect yourself." Ethel wondered as she dabbed her own eyes.

"I can't think about that right now. I'm just too shook up. I can't believe John is gone." Pat's voice was shaky.

"I'm going to miss him so much." Ethel sniffed.

"Me too, I can hardly imagine a world without Jack." Pat started to sob again, "I have to go, see you at the hospital."

"Pat," Ethel whispered, "I love you."

"Love you too, Ethel, we'll get through this somehow." Pat quietly hung up the receiver before the sobbing turned to hysterics.

41

President Johnson stepped off the plane amid a flurry of flash bulbs and microphones shoved close to the podium. He cleared his throat, and with his first lady standing by his side he made the announcement.

"This is a sad time for all people. We have suffered a loss that cannot be weighed. For me, it is a deep personal tragedy. I know the world shares the sorrow that Mrs. Kennedy and her family bear. I will do my best. That is all I can do. I ask for your help and God's."

As the new president gave his brief speech; Robert, Jackie and those who loved John Fitzgerald Kennedy the most quietly took the remains off the back of Air Force One.

McGeorge Bundy had watched the workmen's flurry as they finished the jobs they had come to do and put the offices of the president and his secretary back together. Just as they had taken up the last paint cloth that had protected the new carpeting, Bundy was informed that there was a reporter who wanted an interview.

"Why? Everyone is in Dallas." Bundy asked as he walked with the aide.

Mrs. Lincoln's assistant's face looked stricken as the reporter finished his sentence, "...it's on every news channel and radio station. The president has been shot."

The poor woman went into hysterics when she saw Bundy. Bundy immediately went over to the reporter.

"Turn on all the televisions at once. The president has been shot." She could be heard shouting all over the White House.

Apologizing to the reporter, Bundy was nice yet firm as he asked him to leave them at this deeply upsetting time, "We need to prepare ourselves and our staff for the new president and show him our respect and loyalty."

After giving the protesting reporter to a subordinate to handle, Bundy shook his head at the chaos that was unfolding around him.

It would be a long, long day. However, sadness was not a luxury he could indulge in right now. For the moment, he would be required to be the calm in the ever increasing storm. *Nice timing, Mrs. Kennedy, wanting to have the offices re-carpeted.* Bundy sighed, *never a dull moment.*

"My God, my God, why did you take him now?" Jackie cried on Bobby's shoulder as he held her close and wept silently with her.

"It was awful," she sobbed, "his brains, blood, and hair were just everywhere."

"I know. Jackie, I'm so sorry this happened." Bobby tightened his grip but suddenly she turned on him with an anger that raged deep from within her tortured soul. "Where were you? Why didn't you protect him?"

"Oh, God Jackie, I tried, you don't know how hard I tried." Bobby let her go as she pulled away.

"It's not your fault, Bob, it's mine. I should have had my hair fixed at the beauty salon and then the top would have been up. He was such an easy target, Bob. Back seat, close to the crowd, but he never listens...listened." Jackie crumpled into a chair and sobbed into her hands.

Marilyn had gone to escort the family up to the waiting room, so they could all be together during this horrible time of awaiting the autopsy.

Marilyn stepped to the far end of the room with the other 'employees' as the family greeted each other and grieved. Kenny O'Donnell brought her a cup of lukewarm coffee.

"This is unreal." Marilyn sipped at the tepid drink.

"I can't believe he's gone. You know he used to tell us he would be killed by one of his politicians. I guess he just knew." Kenny motioned for her to sit down on the plastic covered sofa next to him.

"Yes, I guess he did." Marilyn sipped at her coffee only looking up at him occasionally.

"It's heart breaking. He was a very good friend to me." Kenny continued. "Now, Johnson wants me to stay with his administration. I can't."

Bobby had left the family in time to hear this last bit. "Oh, Kenny you must. John would want you to help the policies he has started to live on. You can aide with such grace."

"Are you kidding? You want me to champion that son of a bitch? I'm sure he had something to do with this assassination." Kenny was on his feet. "I'm positive of it."

Bobby put his arm around Kenny's shoulder and walked him a few steps away. Marilyn was still well within ear shot.

"Kenny, that is precisely why you need to be in his office. You can uncover any sinister plot and help get the bastards who did this. We all know it wasn't a lone gunman. This was the work of many, a well-executed plan to kill the president at high noon."

"What? You mean like that movie?" O'Donnell asked.

"Just like the movie. Now you must do this for John's sake. You have to tell Johnson you agree and get him to believe you." Bobby patted his shoulder and hugged him.

"For John," Kenny hugged him back as both men allowed the tears to slip down their cheeks.

Kenny walked away to join some of the other family members as Bobby returned to Marilyn.

"Are you still mad at me?"

"No." Marilyn smiled wanly, "but I must say, I wonder if I've been treated to an Oscar winning performance just as your friend Kenny was."

"What do you mean?"

"John. He told me everything you know, months before I died. I knew of a little plan you had cooked up with him regarding the world tour and then this Dallas trip."

"What?" Bobby stood stunned as she walked away. *Damn it, John!*

Chapter 8

Jack Lancer waited on the edge of his bed watching the door for the cute little brunette nurse to come check on him as she did every night.

"Well, how is my patient doing tonight?" she came into the room with her clipboard and pen. She had unbuttoned enough buttons to reveal a red lacy bra peeking out of her uniform.

"I think I may have a fever Nurse Greta. Maybe you should check to see."

"But Mr. Lancer you haven't had a temperature for weeks now. I didn't bring my thermometer in here with me."

"What kind of a nurse are you?" Jack leaned forward and grabbed her around the waist. She leaned forward, allowing him to burrow his face in her breasts and placed a cool hand on his forehead.

"I'm a very good nurse. I think perhaps you do have a fever. The best thing for you to do is to get out of those pajamas and let me give you a nice bath." She started to undo the first button on his top as he stood up and pulled her against his full length.

"I much prefer a shower, Greta."

"Oh, Mr. Lancer, you're a very naughty patient." She giggled as she pulled him by his collar into the private bathroom and shut the door.

November 23, 1963

Bobby and Ethel climbed the steps to their home in the wee hours of the morning, exhausted and emotionally numb. Heading towards the kitchen, Ethel retrieved the cookies from the cupboard as Bobby put on the kettle for the tea.

"I'm beat." Ethel sat down at the table and watched Bobby piddle around the room aimlessly. "Come sit down, hon."

"I can't. I think it's better if I keep busy." Bobby turned on the tap water and began washing an already clean glass.

Ethel just watched and let him putter around. Grief wasn't new to them. They'd lost more than a few of the family in recent years. Suddenly, he turned to her as water dripped onto the kitchen floor from the rag he held in his hand.

"It's a conspiracy, Ethel. We both know it." he spewed the words in anger.

"Yes." Ethel watched but waited for him to piece it together as he always managed to do.

"Cubans?" Bobby dropped the rag with a splash into the dish water and turned his attention to the whistling tea pot.

"Maybe the Soviets?" Bobby continued to make tea. He filled two cups and brought them to the table.

Ethel sipped her tea, but remained silent as he continued to stew it over.

"That damn Greek bastard had something to do with it or I'm not a Kennedy." Bobby stirred his tea vehemently.

Ethel leaned in close to him and placed a gentle hand on Bobby's cheek. "Hon, you're going to have to calm down a little if you expect to solve this thing. We all know it wasn't Oswald alone."

"No, he was just a dupe. I'll go to my grave knowing that. Thank God the public won't know there was a bullet in his throat too. No way Oswald could have shot him at that angle."

"True and we certainly don't need Johnson getting paranoid there is still an assassin on the loose." Ethel walked over to him. She stroked Bobby's hair back in place over his temple, and held him tight as they both worried silently.

Lyndon Johnson talked loudly to Horace Buzby while Lady Bird was settling comfortably into bed. It was well after midnight and she was exhausted. After Buzby left the bedroom, there was silence but Johnson continued to sit up in bed. With a firm shake of his head, he then reached for the phone and dialed. As the call was answered, Johnson barked into the receiver "I want to meet now, come to the house."

As Johnson spoke, Lady Bird tried to close her eyes. As he hung up the phone, she pleaded "Lyndon, let's go to sleep now. We've had a long day and I want to cuddle with the president." Lady Bird patted the coverlet and giggled like a young bride.

"Not yet, I've just called my aides to come over. I need some answers." Johnson gruffly ignored her request.

"Why, in Heaven's name do you need to do that now? Can't it wait a few more hours? It's not proper to have them in our room."

"Shut up, Birdie, it's my time to shine and I must with all the glory of days past. We can make this a great utopia for America. My aides are on the way."

Aristotle Onassis picked up the phone. He waited, strumming his fingers on the desk in front of him with great impatience.

"Hoffa, where the hell are those tapes?"

"What tapes?"

"You know god damn well which tapes. Spindel installed the recorders for you in Lawford's house and Monroe's house. Where are those tapes? I want them."

"Ask Robert." Hoffa hung up.

Ari sat for several moments, "Damn you, don't you know who I am?"

Jacqueline Kennedy sat at breakfast with a pen and paper in front of her. She jotted notes furiously as she took little bites of the toast on her plate.

An aide came in, "Your sister is on the line."

"Bring the phone here."

"Yes, ma'am."

The phone was brought in with the long phone line trailing behind the aide; the receiver was lifted and handed to Jacqueline.

"Lee, it's about time. I've been trying to reach you since last night." Jackie waved the aide away.

"I'm so sorry about the president." Lee responded, "What can I do."

"Help me repair my image. I had no idea that the American people would respond to me the way they have. It's disconcerting and awkward. They don't like me anymore."

"Well, Jackie, you shouldn't have been publicly sleeping around with Ari and having so much attention brought to the two of you."

"What is done is done. I tried to go with John and be the loving wife. I think that has helped me some."

"But Jackie, we know you weren't the loving wife."

"It's your fault, Lee; if you hadn't stolen the limelight on that tour I wouldn't have felt the need to make my own."

"Oh, no, you don't. You took Ari from me. You know I wanted to marry him and you slept with him anyway."

"We always share our men. You were sleeping with John and I didn't mind." Jackie took a bite of her toast in agitation.

"Jackie, I know you're distraught so we'll talk about this later. What can I do?"

"Get Ari here, I want him in the White House with me."

Frank Sinatra sat alone in his bedroom in Palm Springs, CA. Tapping his lean fingers against the windowsill he suddenly picked up the phone and dialed.

"Hello?"

"Sam? Frank. I need to talk to you. We've been friends a long time now, you cost me my Nevada gaming license and I feel that you owe me the truth on this one."

"What about Boss?" Sam sounded bored.

"I need to know what you had to do with the death of my friend and our president."

Chapter 9

Lee Oswald sat in the interrogation room savoring the attention. "Finally, I'm a star. People know who I am."

The detective looked up from the file folder he had been reading, "A star? Really?"

"Oh yes, I've wanted to prove to the people of this country that the communist way is the best way. Johnson is our best bet to make that happen. I've done everyone a huge favor. Don't you know that Castro is backing Johnson?"

"You don't say?" The detective watched him closely.

You know, Castro wants me in his regime. I'm going to be his right hand man. I know that he'll come and save me."

"I would highly doubt that." The detective wrote the word *crazy* on the folder.

"Yes, they were coming to get me and take me to Cuba to sit with Castro. What a glorious day today will be. I know I'm going to be freed soon."

"Pal, you're going to stand trial for the murders of President Kennedy and Officer Tibbet. The only way you'll ever be free is when you're electrocuted for your crimes."

"We shall see. Poor Marina, she hasn't a clue what I've done, but soon my great accomplishments will be known to her. She'll be so proud and she'll tell our children. She'll finally know what a great soldier I am."

Sam Giancana stood in the alley behind the police station watching as Jack Ruby approached. Jack walked at a brisk purposeful pace.

"Giancana, I just need to know that my family will be taken care of."

"They will Ruby, we've already made arrangements. You take Oswald out right now and we'll make sure they never want for anything."

"I'm only doing this to vindicate my country, and this country. Did you know that my Russia, not this Soviet Union, was a much better place once? Heritage is a funny thing, but I've made a new heritage here in America and I loved Kennedy. I will gladly spend my last few months in prison to kill that bastard Oswald."

The reporters began lining up, waiting for Oswald to be moved. Giancana stepped forward and in a rare move, held out his hand to Jack Ruby.

"To our deal," They shook hands and Ruby started to move toward the reporters.

"Don't forget to take care of Marina. She never knew I was her uncle twice removed, but she deserves to live her life without the stigma of her insane husband hanging over her head. Once I kill him, you'll ensure that she gets everything she needs, right?"

"Yes. We'll make sure." Giancana watched the reporters gather along the hallways. "How are you going to get in there?"

"Giancana you're not too smart are you? I'll simply hand them free drink coupons for my bar." Ruby held up a fistful of paper. "I'll be fast friends with them all in no time." Ruby smiled and headed into the building.

Bobby Kennedy picked up the phone that never stopped ringing. He'd just put the receiver down when the blasted thing rang again. Impatient to get to bed, he answered with gruffness, "Hello."

"Bobby, this is Frank Sinatra, I just called to give you my condolences and let you know how much I loved him too."

Bobby softened, "Thanks, Frank. My entire family appreciates it."

"You know," Frank continued, "I'll do everything I can to help you solve this thing."

"I may need you to stand by that. I know who your friends are."

"Yes, you do. Just know that I'm grieving with you and your family." Frank sighed and hung up.

Jacqueline Kennedy escorted the photographer into the Oval Office. "I want pictures taken of this room and his secretary's so that we can show what it would have looked like if he had returned."

"Yes, Mrs. Kennedy."

"Hurry and take the pictures before the new president would like to get in his new office."

Marilyn walked into the den where Bobby was staring at the phone.

"How are you?" Marilyn asked as she sat down in the chair across from him.

"Doing okay considering..." Bobby leaned toward her.

"I know. The death was awful, gruesome even. I can't believe she climbed out to retrieve the brain matter." Marilyn reached over and patted his hand.

"Shock. She was in shock. I don't know what I would do in that situation." Bobby tapped his fingers on the phone, "I wonder how I would handle it if it were Ethel. My God, I can't imagine losing that woman."

"You are blessed to have such a wonderful marriage and a deep love for each other. I've wanted that my whole life." Marilyn stood to go. "When are you going to talk to him?"

"Talk to whom?" Bobby looked up startled.

"Jack in the Alps." Marilyn walked away before he could answer.

Chapter 10

Marina Oswald sat with her neighbor watching the caisson of President Kennedy's casket from the White House to the Capitol Rotunda. They were watching NBC's live coverage of the procession as the cameras shifted to the transfer of the prisoner in Dallas.

Tom Petit reports, "The accused is being transferred from the Dallas City Jail to the Dallas County Jail."

Lee Harvey Oswald's right hand was handcuffed to the escorting detective as he made his way down the steps.

Jack Ruby stood among the reporters trying to make his way to the forefront. He had his gun ready in the pocket of his jacket. *Justice for all. . .*

The officers escorted Lee Harvey Oswald to the basement. Oswald kept ranting about police brutality until they reached the reporters.

Oswald lifted his free hand in a communist salute, smiled for the cameras and was promptly shot dead by Jack Ruby.

Amid the flash bulbs, Ruby stood with the smoking gun in his hand as the officers tackled him and slapped cuffs on his wrists.

"He's been shot! He's been shot! Lee Oswald has been shot!" shouted the reporter, "There is absolute panic. Pandemonium has broken out."

Marina watched as her husband crumpled to the ground in a heap. She promptly fainted, sliding off the plastic covered couch.

Lyndon Johnson stood in the middle of the Oval Office directing his belongings to their new homes. He was euphoric, almost giddy as he placed his things around him. Lady Bird stood by the window watching him. His aides came in and out in quick succession to do his bidding.

Kenny O'Donnell walked into the office as the move was in progress. He surveyed the room with some sadness and then approached Johnson.

"Mr. President, I'm with you." Kenny held out his hand.

"Thank you, Mr. O'Donnell. It is most important that we present America with a united front in the White House. I appreciate that you have reconsidered." Mr. Johnson smiled in genuine pleasure.

"I'm merely here to assure that Mr. Kennedy's executive orders are carried out, Mr. Johnson. Let the American public think what they will."

Kenny walked out of the Oval Office leaving Johnson standing with his mouth open.

Jacqueline Kennedy sat with a reporter extolling the virtues of her deceased husband. "Camelot. That's what we were building. John so much wanted to be a modern day Camelot here in America."

Lee sat in the opposite chair watching her sister bewitch the reporter and spin her disaster into success. *She's a smart bitch, I'll give her that. Everyone will be diverted by this great idea she's spinning about John, and they will completely forget they hate her.*

"Operator, I have a person to person call for Robert Kennedy."

"Hang on operator, I'll get my husband. Who shall I tell him is calling?" Ethel asked.

"Jack Lancer." The operator responded.

"Jack Lancer?" Ethel puzzled, "Just a moment."

Bobby looked up from the paper he had been reading in the dining room as Ethel held her hand over the receiver.

"It's for you honey. Jack Lancer."

Bobby's face paled as he heard the name. "I'll take it in the den. I don't want to be disturbed and make sure no one picks up this line. It's a matter of national security."

Ethel watched in confusion as he left. "Hold on operator, he's coming now."

Aristotle Onassis walked into the White House and was greeted by Lee and Jacqueline. He took Jackie in his arms and held her firmly, a huge smug grin on his face.

"I would love to say I'm sorry for the loss of your husband, but that would be a blatant lie." Ari hugged her for another moment before he let her go. "Now we shall let the mourning period begin, but it should be understood that you will be my wife."

"Robert Kennedy." Bobby listened while the line crackled and popped. After a series of clicks the caller came through loud and clear.

"Bobby? Bobby what the hell did you do? You were supposed to save him." As the frantic voice crackled over the line Bobby sank into his chair.

"Jack, I tried, God knows I tried. What a disaster." Bobby laid his head in his free hand and hugged the receiver close to the other ear.

"But Bob, what am I supposed to do?"

"I don't know John, I haven't gotten that far. Obviously, you can't come back now. I mean the whole world watched Jackie crawl over the trunk to get the scalp."

"Then what do I do?"

"Things aren't exactly calm here."

"But Jackie thinks I've been killed, my kids are devastated that daddy's gone and the entire world is babbling about my brains being splattered all over the back of the limo!"

"Calm down, Jack, I can't think with you yelling like that."

Jacqueline knelt by the casket with John-John and Carolyn. Suddenly Carolyn kissed the side of the casket and began to cry, "Daddy, don't be in heaven, come back to me and my pony."

Jacqueline quickly took her daughter by the hand, picked up John-John and led them out of the room.

One of the guards opened the door as they passed and wiped a tear from his own eye once they had gone by.

Chapter 11

Marilyn dried her eyes as the caisson rolled by holding the remains of the 'president.' Carolyn stood beside John Jr. who had just saluted the casket of his father. The photographers were snapping pictures of him in rapid fire succession. Marilyn gathered the Robert Kennedy children up and walked them away from the display.

Ethel caught up with them and took the baby out of her arms. Just as Marilyn removed the veil that had covered her face for the occasion a stray photographer popped a bulb in their faces and took off.

"Show some respect, won't you?" Marilyn called after the retreating figure.

Ethel sighed, "You'd think they'd understand our grief."

"They don't. Anything for a scoop or story someone else may miss."

"Try not to forget, they are grieving as well." Ethel reached over and patted Marilyn's arm.

"Yes, of course. I'm not used to the paparazzi anymore." Marilyn hugged Ethyl.

"I'm going to try and catch up with Bobby. See you at the house."

Marilyn took the baby out of Ethel's arms and smiled at her. "I'll get them all settled at home and see you later."

Fidel Castro turned off the television set. He sighed and lit a cigar. "Touching the way the Americans have glorified their president. It is most unfortunate that they have no idea how close to war with us they truly are."

Sam Giancana smiled as he blew a puff of smoke in the air. "Have you talked to the Soviets?"

"Yes, we are all waiting to see what Johnson does. If he fulfills his obligations, we will not have to go to war. We shall wait and see." Castro leaned back in the leather chair, relaxed and confident. "He is very concerned about our amigos and the friends of Robert Kennedy. I don't think there will be any trouble from the new commander and chief."

"And Khrushchev?" Sam repeated the question

Castro simply laughed, put out his cigar, and took a sip of his drink. "All in good time, my friend, all in good time."

Marilyn had the seven older children holding hands and following her progress down the crowded avenue through the throngs of mourners. As she got to the curb she heard an ear-piercing scream from one of the girls.

"What's wrong?" She turned, still holding Christopher in her arms.

"It's Mary Kerry. Someone grabbed her and she's gone."

"HELP! Kerry's been kidnapped! HELP!" Marilyn took off running in the direction the child was pointing.

Pat rushed up to the rest of her nieces and nephews, gathered them close and grabbed Christopher out of Marilyn's arms as she ran past.

Peter caught up to her, and he and Marilyn were in hot pursuit of the kidnapper as young Kerry screamed for all she was worth.

One of the secret service agents broke ranks, leapt ahead of Marilyn and Peter catching up to the kidnapper.

"Stop! Put the child down."

The kidnapper stopped but didn't turn around. He held the child tighter as she screamed, "Daddy! Daddy! Save me." Hysterical sobs emitted from her throat as the agent stepped a little closer to them. The kidnapper took a small step away

"Go ahead and move asshole! I'd love to shoot you." The agent commanded as the man turned to face him with a terrified four-year-old girl pummeling her tiny fists against his neck and face. "Put the child down!" The agent waited for a split second, "NOW!"

Realizing defeat, the man let the child go and she raced to Marilyn's outstretched arms sobbing hysterically. Marilyn grabbed her up and held her close.

The agent roughly hand-cuffed the kidnapper as other agents rushed to the scene. The agents led the man away as little Kerry cried on Marilyn's shoulder. Marilyn, trying to comfort the child, was crying herself as she headed back to the family.

"Ma'am, we'll come get a statement from you at the house. Take the little ones home." The agent ushered the family away from the scene; then returned to the business of dealing with the kidnapper.

Jack Lancer, aka John Fitzgerald Kennedy, paced restlessly around the enclosed area of the hospital. The news articles relating to his 'death' were laid out across a picnic table proclaiming the world's grief and terror at the "Assassination of the United States President."

With such titles as, "Who is next?" or "Why JFK?" the cries of the news reporters rang loudly in the ears of everyone worldwide.

"What a fucking mess!" Jack picked up a cigarette and lit it; he puffed a few times, and threw it down on the snow covered ground in his agitation.

His 'funeral' had been earlier in the day. The image of his young family going through the motions of that long service would not leave him. "I'm so sorry Jackie. It wasn't supposed to be like this."

A nurse came out onto the patio with a pair of fur lined gloves, "Mr. Lancer? You should put these on or come inside. There is another snow coming soon."

He looked up, nodded, and took the gloves from her. Before he put them on he swiped the back of his hand across his eyes.

"Is everything all right, Mr. Lancer?"

"Fine. I guess I'm just a little sad." He nodded toward the papers strewn out on the table.

"Yes, I would imagine that it's awful to know your president has been killed. Is there anything I can do for you sir?" She batted her eye lashes at him and smiled coyly.

"Not tonight, Greta, but thanks for your concern."

Pouting, "Don't stay out here too long, it's going to get very cold out." She swayed her hips as she returned to the warmth of the hospital.

J. Edgar Hoover sat behind the mahogany desk reading with great interest the transcripts on the JFK and Marilyn Monroe affair. It was better by far than any racy novel. The secrets and sex were exhilarating to him. His dreams of a threesome had shattered with their deaths, but now as he avidly read, those dreams could at least be somewhat real for the moment.

His spies had done an excellent job in tapping into the wire taps that Kennedy himself had had installed in the Oval Office. Now completely engrossed, Hoover nearly fell out of the chair when the shrill sound of the phone ringing pulled him away from the sordid affairs of JFK.

"Hoover" he barked, "this better be worth my time."

"Frank Sturgis, chief, I have some information about the KGB that you need to know about."

"Not now, Sturgis, I'll meet you tomorrow."

"But chief, this may not wait."

"What is it?" Hoover marked the place in the file with his pen and turned his attention to the phone call.

"A KGB agent, Yuri Nosenko, wants to meet with the head of the CIA."

"Why the hell do I care about that right now?" Hoover pulled his glasses off of his nose and threw them on the desk.

"He says he has information about Oswald that we need to know."

"They always say that, Sturgis, they are prima donnas." Hoover rubbed his temples with both hands, balancing the receiver on his shoulder.

"I don't think so this time chief. He says that Oswald was a dupe in a much bigger plot and you are a fool if you don't talk to him."

"Okay Ms. Baker, I think we have enough." The police detective closed his notepad and stood up, "If we have any further questions we'll contact you or Mr. Kennedy."

Ethel had returned from the nursery to finish her interview with the detective. "Please tell me, officer, what that maniac was thinking taking my baby?"

"He wanted to warn the Kennedy's ma'am. This is not the first or last time an attempt will be made on your family. Consider yourself lucky that we were able to catch him. You can be certain he will be held accountable for his actions."

"Warn us? What do you mean?"

"Mrs. Kennedy your brother-in-law has just been killed and your husband is leading the crusade to find out by whom. Surely you didn't think you'd be safe?" The officer frowned at her kindly.

"Well then we'll need to beef up our protection from the secret service." Ethel shook the officer's hand and led him from the room. "Thank you for your prompt attention to our situation."

"We're just doing our jobs, ma'am. I'm sorry for your loss. Please convey my condolences to your husband. You and your family stay on high alert." The officer stood at the open front door and disappeared into the dark cold night.

Chapter 12

Frank stared into the blackness through the window in his bedroom where he'd been for days. The bottle of Jack Daniels was nearly empty.

Frank got up, swayed a little and held on to the dresser for support. As he headed for the bedroom door, it opened. Frank Jr. walked in carrying a steak with green beans on a tray.

"Dad, you really need to eat something and sober up."

Frank sat down on the bed, ran a shaky hand through his hair and sneered at his son. "I don't want anything right now."

"Look Dad, we all know this is devastating to you but you can't live in here forever. Try to eat something and pull yourself together."

"Oh and you think you know something at the ripe old age of what, twenty?" Frank glared at his son.

"I'm nineteen. And yes, I do know something. The president would be ashamed of you right now. If you can do anything to help the family, you should." Frank Jr. held the tray out but his father just ignored it.

"Well, you can give me credit for at least one thing. I didn't raise a fool."

Frank Jr. handed his dad the tray and sat down on the bed beside him. "No, you didn't and you ain't one either." They both chuckled.

"You know how I hate improper grammar." Frank picked up the fork and knife to cut the steak.

"Yes, but it made you smile. Now be a good man and eat all of your dinner."

Frank chewed his steak for a moment, "Thanks. I'll do what's right by them, make no mistake about it."

Jacqueline, Bobby and Ethel all sat around the dining room table watching John-John open the presents for his third birthday.

"What a day." Bobby put his arm securely around Jackie, a comforting gesture, "I can't imagine a worse day for a birthday party. We just buried his father this morning and someone tried to take our Kerry."

"We promised him a party. I couldn't break a promise that Jack had made to him." Jackie leaned into Bobby's shoulder and wiped away a tear.

"Why did you invite that bastard?" Bobby asked as Aristotle handed a gift to John Jr.

"I needed someone to comfort me and help me through my grief." Jackie sat up effectively pulling away from Bobby's warmth.

"I'm here to help you through your grief; you don't need that Greek bastard to further smear your reputation."

November 28, 1963

The sound of laughter could be heard throughout the compound. Castro clapped and slapped his leg in jubilance, "That's right, Mr. President. Give a speech for your stupid American holiday."

"Fidel, my darling, what is going on in here?" Marita came into the room with a tray of snacks and drinks. She set it on the table as he turned his attention to her, while the television droned on in the background.

Castro mocked the words he'd just heard, "...determined that from this nightmare of tragedy we shall move toward a new American greatness."

"Who said that?" Marita asked as she handed him a glass half full of port and a huge sandwich.

"Johnson, he is indeed on our side as he should be after the favor we've granted to him." Castro grabbed Marita and pulled her onto his lap and kissed her soundly. "He has signed NSAM 273 to escalate the Vietnam conflict into war a few days ago and now this noble speech!" Castro kissed her again as he groped her breast.

Marilyn sat at the kitchen table; a steaming cup of hot chocolate and piece of pumpkin pie in front of her. She played with her fork as Bobby came in.

"I got the kids down, they were exhausted. What a horrible few days." Marilyn took a small bite of pie while he poured out coffee.

Coming over to the table he sat down across from her as he dipped his finger into the whipped cream on top of her plate.

"Hey! Get your own." Marilyn pulled her plate closer to her as she smiled at him.

"I know I don't tell you very often," Bobby began, but stopped at the incredulous expression on her face, "Okay, never, but you are really great with the kids and we're lucky to have you." He smiled a broad grin.

Marilyn eyed him with suspicion, "Thanks Bobby, but..."

"But the elephant in the room is that you need to go to Jack." Bobby held her gaze until she looked down at her plate.

"Why? He deserves what he has gotten." She gazed back at him, "I know I should feel more empathy for him but I don't. I'm over him now. He can just stay in Switzerland and make a new life for himself." Marilyn scooped up a huge fork of whipped cream with a little bit of pie and shoved it into her mouth.

"Yes, I know you have closed the book on him but that's not why I need you to go. You have to catch him up on the politics that have been going on since he left for his surgery and help him figure out who was really behind the assassination."

"What?" Marilyn put her fork down, "Why me? I can't go. No, just send Kenny." She picked up her coffee and swirled the contents around in her cup.

"I can't send him he's going to be working with Johnson as my spy in the Oval Office." Bobby watched her tap her fingers restlessly on the table for a moment before he continued, "You're the only one I can trust."

"Does anyone know he's alive but you and me?"

70

"I told Kenny because we needed someone on the inside close to Johnson." Bobby played with a bowl of sugar on the table.

"And that's it? Just the three of us know?"

"Yes, not even Ethel knows. Come on, I need you." Bobby laid his hand across hers on the table. "Please."

"Why Mr. Kennedy, it's not like you to beg." Marilyn smiled and removed her hand. "I always thought that John was the charming one, but you know how to flash the charm too, don't you?"

"Is that a 'yes'?" Bobby leaned back in his chair and picked up the coffee mug, watching her over the rim as he sipped.

"Do I have a choice?"

"No."

"When do I leave?" Marilyn stood up, took her plate to the sink and waited on his response.

Yuri Nosenko sat on the uncomfortable metal chair in the cold visiting room of the Dallas jail waiting with a great deal of impatience for his few minutes with the inmate.

The door opened and Jack Ruby, handcuffed and heavily guarded, entered the windowless room. The guard seated Ruby, snapped another set of cuffs to the metal loop on the metal table and pushed him into the metal chair with unneeded roughness. Ruby grunted as his rump hit the ice-cold seat.

"You have five minutes." The guard left the room and stood outside the door peering in through the tiny window where only one eye could be seen from Nosenko's vantage point.

Ruby broke the silence, "How did you get in here?"

"I have my ways. At the moment, I'm a CIA agent here at the request of Hoover." Nosenko chortled.

"The dumb bastards bought that?" Ruby shook his head. "Why are you here?"

"Insurance. I need to see what you plan to tell them at your trial."

Ruby looked Nosenko squarely in the eye, "Now you go back and tell that little shit, Hoover that we all know I did it for Jackie and the kids...maybe I ought to forget this silly story that I'm telling, and get on the stand AND tell the TRUTH."

"Are you threatening the establishment?" Nosenko stood, his chair scraping loudly on the concrete floor.

"Not exactly, I just wanted my position understood. I took the fall but I need to be respected and treated well for my last few years."

"Very good, Ruby."

"My family?"

"They are set up nicely. We should all live so well." Nosenko shook his head.

"Tell the CIA thank you." Ruby smiled.

"Anyone in particular I should thank?"

"Eduardo. Oh, and tell Marita I said 'hello'."

"Castro's woman?" Nosenko asked incredulous.

"Of course, how many Marita's do you know?"

"Well my little widow, what are your plans now?" Ari stroked Jackie's hair away from her face and planted a light kiss in the nape of her neck. Jackie snuggled closer and pulled the covers tighter around them both.

"Now? As in right this minute now?" Jackie put her arm around his waist and hugged him. "Well, right now I'm just laying here enjoying the warmth of great loving."

Aristotle chuckled and kissed the top of her head. "Now, as in the near future, not right this moment."

"I shall go back to journalism and tell the world what a great and wonderful man the late president was. I won't ever tell them what a selfish lover he was or how I despised his touch."

"Endearing, my darling, you build your fantasy Camelot world into whatever you need it to be, but don't forget I'm waiting." Ari closed his eyes and slept.

Chapter 13

Howard Hughes lay on the bed in his cramped little room looking for any signs of light. Or was it night? *If it was night, there'd be no light. Why is everything so hard?* He forced himself to be calm as he tried to focus on the past few days. *It's not that I want company, people are so germy. But no one has been to see me in days. Or, was it just yesterday the man in the suit had asked me if I wanted to see Jean?* Thoughts floated in and out of his disturbed mind. *Flying. I miss flying. Or, have I just been up in my H-1 racer?*

The door opened and in walked a well-dressed man in an expensive looking suit. He was followed by two other men who had masks over their faces. *That's good, keep your germs to yourself.* Howard started to get up but the masked men held him down while the nicely dressed gentleman administered a shot into his shoulder.

"Would you like anything Mr. Hughes?" he asked.

"Where's your mask?" Howard's voice was inaudible as he hid his face behind his hands.

"Now Howard, you know I do not have germs." The man smiled, "I'll be back to check in a while, maybe then you'll want something to eat."

"Eat? Is it time to eat? I must wash my hands." Howard rose and turned to the sink in the corner. He visibly shook as the panic over took him. "Where's the soap?" he cried.

"Calm yourself," the man patted his arm, "I will bring you some soap."

Jacqueline drug herself out of the warmth of the bed, crossed the room and picked up the phone ringing in the hallway as she closed the bedroom door behind her.

"Hello?"

"Jackie, thank God! What are we going to do to fix this?"

"Who is this?"

"It's John, your husband."

"Is this a cruel prank? You realize this phone is tapped." Jackie leaned against the wall as the fatigue of the last week sank fully into her bones.

"It's also our own private line, Jackie. I swear this is John."

"John is dead."

"No, I'm not. I'm in the Alps. I wanted to have my back fixed."

"Liar. Bastard."

"Jackie, remember that vacation we took after our honeymoon? You got so sunburned that I had to rub aloe vera on you for a week? Your back peeled in the shape of the liberty bell. Remember that?"

"No one knows that story." Jackie allowed herself to slide down the wall and sit on the lush carpeting. "I never told anyone."

"Nor did I, Jacks, it's really me."

December 8, 1963

Frankie Sinatra, Jr. and John Foss sat eating dinner at the Lodge before their set was to begin at Harrah's in Lake Tahoe. They were appearing with the Tommy Dorsey Band that night.

A knock sounded at the door, "I have a package for Mr. Sinatra."

Frankie opened the door and found a thirty-eight revolver pointed in his face.

"Get down on the floor," the man in the ski mask pushed his way into the room.

Frankie and John both lay down on their stomachs, heads down, waiting silently.

"Hands behind your backs," the man instructed.

The young men complied without a word. Suddenly they were being blindfolded as their hands were taped. Another man had entered the room as they lay on the floor. He took their wallets and made Frankie stand up.

He pushed him roughly and Frankie stumbled, caught himself and stood up straight facing his captors.

"Go get your coat and shoes," the man holding the gun instructed Frankie as he cut the tape from Frankie's wrists. Frankie did what he was told as the other man leaned down to John.

"Don't make any noise for at least ten minutes. If we don't make it to Sacramento, there will be trouble."

The men drug Frankie out the door and into the car, speeding away into the night.

December 10, 1963

Marilyn stepped out of the taxi onto the ice-covered sidewalk at the hotel in Geneva, Switzerland. The cabbie opened the trunk and began unloading her suitcases onto the trolley cart brought out by the bell boy. Marilyn tipped the cab driver then quickly walked into the warmth of the hotel.

"May I help you?" the manager asked.

"Yes, I have a reservation. Zelda Zonk."

"Right this way Ms. Zonk we have been expecting you. Your party is waiting in the restaurant." The manager waved her toward the café with a flourish.

"Let him wait. I'm exhausted and need a few minutes to freshen up. You can let Mr. Lancer know that I'm here and will join him in half an hour."

Agents Latimer and Stansel reported to President Johnson promptly at ten a.m. The secretary sat them in the Oval Office.

"Check this out." Stansel looked around the opulent, newly redecorated room.

"Exactly what you would expect of the president's office, Jacqueline Kennedy has exquisite taste." Latimer glanced around then stood as Johnson entered the room.

Stansel jumped up, nearly knocking the serving tray off of the table.

"Mr. President, I'm Agent Latimer and this is Agent Stansel."

"Sit down gentlemen and get comfortable. Help yourself to some coffee." Johnson sat down in a high wing backed chair across from them, crossed his leg and swung his booted foot.

"What can we do for you, Mr. President?" Stansel asked as he added sugar to his delicate little china cup.

"It has come to my attention that you two were involved in the business with JFK and Marilyn Monroe. What were the results of that investigation?"

Latimer leaned forward, "What do you mean, Mr. President? Specifically speaking, that is."

Johnson leaned forward as well and pointed his long finger at the agents, "Don't toy with me, Latimer, was it? I eat men like you for breakfast."

"I can't answer such a vague question, Mr. President, with all due respect." Latimer picked up a tiny sliver of coffee cake and popped it in his mouth.

"Did Ms. Monroe know any political secrets?"

"Not that we've uncovered." Latimer leaned back in his chair and sipped the steaming hot coffee.

Stansel took his cue from his partner and remained silent. He continued to watch the president with careful consideration.

"You know that you have an obligation to your country to tell me the truth?" Johnson shifted in his massive chair, angling to intimidate the men.

"Yes, Mr. President." Latimer rose to leave, setting his coffee cup on the table. "Is there anything else we can do for you?"

Frustrated Johnson stood as well, "If you do remember something or find anything useful in the files, it is your duty as an agent to inform me immediately."

"Yes sir, Mr. President. We'll let you know." Latimer and Stansel left the room and headed down the hall. After a few minutes, Latimer audibly sighed.

Stansel glanced at his partner, "The Attorney General needs to know about this."

Chapter 14

Aristotle Onassis stepped out of the limo in front of the posh restaurant on Hollywood Blvd and motioned for the doorman to let him in. Robert Allen sat at a table near the windows awaiting him.   Aristotle marched over to the table and sat down before the host could even greet him.

"All right Robert, where are they?"

"I don't have them anymore."

"Don't have them? There better be a god damned good reason you don't have them anymore."

"I...."

Aristotle stopped Robert before he could get a sentence out. His famous Greek temper in full throttle, face red and cheeks puffing, "You sorry son of a bitch, those tapes mean everything to me. You are an insufferable buffoon. I'll kill you, you insolent bastard."

Robert sipped at his wine as the Greek ranted and raved, apparently unconcerned at the tirade being spewed onto his head. When Aristotle finally sat down, Robert placed his glass gently on the table, wiped his mouth with his napkin, and stood up.

"Onassis, you'd catch more flies with honey than that vinegar you spit. I don't have the tapes because Robert Kennedy had his men take them from me. It was quite a fight but he won. He always wins."

President Johnson chuckled as he heard Jacqueline's voice answer his call.

"Mr. President to what do I owe the pleasure of this call?" Jackie sighed, as she prepared herself for this conversation.

"You promised me you would come see me before you moved out of the White House. Do I need to remind you?" Johnson wheeled.

"I've been really busy with the move. It's been a rough month or so."

"Well, little dahlin' that is not an excuse. Perhaps Papa needs to spank you?"

"Mr. President, I don't believe that will be necessary. You're not my Papa and I have never needed spanked."

Johnson laughed in a loud guffaw, "You do tickle my fancy, you poor little widow. I'm sure you're in need of a man to keep you safe and secure."

"I've got my family, don't worry about me. I will try and come visit you and *Mrs.* Johnson soon." Jackie lit a cigarette as her shoulders began to tighten.

"I'll declare you are harder to rope into a meeting than a bull. Don't make me have you arrested and brought in for punishment, little lady." Johnson cackled out loud at his own joke.

"Again, Mr. President, I will do my best to see you and your lovely wife soon. Please make sure you give her my regards. I really must go pick up Caroline, school is out in a few moments." Jackie blew out a breath leaving smoke hanging in the air.

"Okay, but little dahlin' you must hold to your promises." Johnson hung up long after the buzz of the dead connection began in his ear.

Marilyn checked her appearance in the lobby mirror, sucked in her breath, then blew it out slowly, before she entered the restaurant. She had meticulously dressed in her best outfit, fixed her hair in the familiar movie starlet style and put on her face with extreme care. Oh, yes, she was woman and she was ready to confront this situation. Armed in her best fur coat and favorite high heels, she knew she was a Hollywood star if only for a moment.

As she turned from the mirror the hotel clerk smiled in appreciation of her beauty. "You look like that star, Ms. Zonk, you know, Marilyn Monroe."

"Thank you!" Marilyn giggled coyly and blew him a kiss. She turned on her heel and walked into the restaurant oozing her famous charm.

Jackie hung up the phone and called Lee.

"You won't believe what that arrogant jack ass is saying to me now." Jackie blurted as soon as Lee had answered.

"Oh, Jacks, you and your men," Lee giggled, "Who's causing the problem this time?"

"Johnson. Oh, if only I could give him a true piece of my mind."

"Well, you know you can't do that but I could put a word out to Ari and have him deal with it."

"No, don't do that, I've got enough to deal with. He'd just pull some sneaky political trick which would incite more of Johnson's wrath. No thanks. Maybe I'll just move to New York."

John watched the beautiful blonde sway into the room. She stopped and looked about with an oddly familiar expression on her face. As she looked directly at him the dim light changed and lit her profile as the full truth registered on his shocked face.

"Oh, there you are darling." Marilyn swept across the floor and waited for him to pull out her chair. The waiter hustled forward and slid her wrap from thin shoulders, revealing an elegant evening gown with a very low cut neckline. Diamonds glittered on her long neck and as she settled herself John tried to regain his composure.

Pleased with his confusion, Marilyn leaned forward, took his hand and rubbed her finger over his in an old familiar gesture. "Hi Lover, you don't look so good."

John gulped, took another look at her and gulped again.

"What's wrong, honey? Cat got your tongue?" Marilyn let go of his hand and leaned back in her chair.

The waiter came up and set down a glass of water and a basket of rolls. He smiled and handed her the wine list but didn't leave.

"You may go." John's voice sounded rusty.

"Please, if you could give us a few minutes?" Marilyn smiled at the waiter who nearly melted into the background to obey her wishes.

"My God, Marilyn...I thought...I mean... my God, Marilyn. How?"

"You of all people should know good and well 'how'. Aren't you dead as well? It's not so difficult to fake death, after all." Marilyn dropped the simpering lover act as she answered. "However, I'm 'dead' partly because of you and your politics. But you, you're 'dead' because of your own stupidity."

"This is crazy." John ran his hand over the top of his head in an agitated gesture, "I don't know what to say." He sipped his water and nearly choked on it.

"That's fine. I have plenty to say and you can listen while you figure it out. If you hadn't been such a chicken shit the summer of 1962 I wouldn't be dead. You forced my hand. How in the hell did you expect to push me off by having your brother come and tell me to leave you alone?" Marilyn paused for a moment but didn't give him time to answer.

"I'll tell you how, because you couldn't risk your political reputation or your presidency by being a mature boy, about high school age, and telling me yourself that you no longer had an interest in me. Instead you decided it would be best to send your little brother to do your dirty work. Bad idea." Marilyn lit a cigarette and held up a hand for silence while she puffed.

"Do you know I went through hell because of you? Arrogant idiot, you weren't dealing with a mousy little girl who hadn't a clue how to deal with a man. Oh no, sir. I knew how to deal with you and that's why you're such a pussy coward."

John finally found his voice, "Marilyn please, it wasn't like that. I loved you. I still do."

"Really? Is that how you show a woman you love her? You cut the phone line you had for me. You refused to talk to me or take my calls or telegrams. Pretty boy pussy."

"It was the best thing to keep it hushed up. Why didn't you just shut up? It was all for Teddy so he could win the senate seat in Massachusetts."

"You broke it off with me over politics? That is low."

"No, I only wanted to put you off for a year or so. My presidency needed a boost. So you were cut off. I sent Bobby to tell you."

"Why? I deserved an explanation from you personally because I wasn't just another bimbo or a two-bit blonde whore. But you never gave it to me did you?"

She waited for an answer but he just sat there, "Were you aware of why I wanted to talk to you in person? Why it was so urgent?"

John just shook his head in the negative, looking like a little boy being scolded for forgetting to complete his homework assignment.

"Because, John, I was pregnant with your baby." Marilyn paused and let that sink in. "I wanted to let you know I'd be in Mexico for a week. I guess it was just too much to expect that you would be sympathetic to my problem."

John's mouth dropped open, "I had no idea."

"Men never do, but you might have if you would have had the balls to talk to me."

Chapter 15

"No Mr. President, I don't have any real findings yet." Mr. Warren shifted nervously on the seat in front of Lyndon Johnson's massive desk. The president towered over him.

"We set up your commission, Mr. Warren in good faith that you would quickly find out who shot Kennedy. We need to keep further threats against our government away."

"You mean yourself, of course, Mr. President?"

"Yes, exactly, so figure it out. I don't take my personal safety lightly. I carry my own gun and I'll kill the bastards myself."

Kenny O'Donnell was waiting impatiently for the meeting to end with LBJ and Mr. Warren when Lady Bird flittered into the inner office agitated.

"Good afternoon, Mrs. Johnson, he's in a meeting and you can't go in there." Kenny smiled at her, "Would you like to sit down and wait?"

"I'm far too worried to do that. Perhaps you could help me since he's specifically asked you to stay on for his presidency. I bet you know how serious I should have taken this comment."

"Please do sit down and we'll figure it out together." Kenny himself took the secretary's chair and sat at the desk. Lady Bird fluttered into the wing back chair in front of him.

"Now, what is this all about?" Kenny leaned toward her in a friendly gesture.

"Well, I haven't told a soul because Lyndon said I should keep my mouth shut or we would be killed so I did, keep my mouth shut, that is, but I'm really worried they'll get him now that President Kennedy is gone." Lady Bird's speech flittered like a sparrow diving for worms.

"Who?" Kenny patted the hand she had placed on the corner of the desk in sympathy.

"That Greek...hurricane?" Lady Bird looked confused.

"Tycoon?" Kenny prompted, "You mean Aristotle Onassis?"

"Yes, that sounds right. I overheard every word on the plane." Lady Bird placed her hand over her heart.

"Mrs. Johnson, I'm trying my best to understand where you are going with this. Will you tell me where and what plane?" Kenny smiled, stood up and poured her a cup of coffee from the credenza next to the desk. He held up the cream and she nodded affirmative, he added some to her cup then plopped in two lumps of sugar.

"Oh, thank you. This should help settle my nerves. It is so nice to talk to you about this. It's been scaring the daylights out of me since the assassination took place. It happened on

Air Force One while they were loading the remains of President Kennedy." She took a sip of her coffee and relaxed a little.

"Please go on, Mrs. Johnson, I'm sure it was nothing to worry about and I'll be able to help you." Kenny had written Onassis on a yellow legal pad and had a pen poised in his hand.

"He said to Lyndon, my husband you know, he said, 'There was no conspiracy, Oswald was a lone nut assassin. Get it Lyndon? Otherwise, Air Force One might have an unfortunate accident on the flight back to Washington.' It scared me to death and I was already very upset that Mrs. Kennedy refused to clean herself up for the swearing in." Lady Bird sipped her coffee, sighing in relief.

"There, there, Mrs. Johnson, I'll look into it and you need not worry about it anymore. We've got around the clock security watching the president and it won't happen again." Kenny smiled at her warmly and finished jotting down his notes.

"So, this is where we stand at the moment." Latimer handed the report to Bobby.

"The president is looking into my brother and Marilyn? Why? What possible reason would he have now that they are both dead?" Bobby thumbed through the report as Latimer prepared to leave the attorney general's office.

"He didn't really say but I wonder if Johnson thought Marilyn Monroe knew about his plans to make Vietnam a war." Latimer had put on his overcoat and began buttoning it up.

"Keep him guessing. You got that?" Bobby tossed the report on his desk and shook hands with Latimer

"Yes, I've got it. My loyalty is to you and your family, Mr. Kennedy." Latimer returned the handshake.

"Loyalty is something we could use right now."

"Bobby?" Frank Sinatra asked into the receiver.

"What do you need, Frank?"

"My son has been kidnapped. I don't know what to do. Can you help me find him?"

"I'll try. What do you know?"

"They called, but they don't know how much money they want, where to meet them or when they want it."

"Okay, Frank, I'll send someone over to help you out. We'll handle this together."

"Thank you, Bobby. I knew I could count on you."

Jack Lancer watched as Marilyn stormed away. He sighed and leaned back in his chair. She hadn't even stayed to eat and her rage was apparent in every stride she took away from him.

"Fine!"

The waiter appeared at his elbow, "Is everything all right, sir?"

"Yes. A bottle of scotch, please." Jack sighed and lit his cigar.

The waiter had hustled off while Jack took the first few puffs on the cigar. Jack closed his eyes and his mind wandered back to the disturbing telephone call to Jackie.

"Dead, do you hear me?" Jackie whispered with icy calm. "I have worked hard to build this fairy-tale, Camelot, in order to restore my reputation. You are dead, you will stay dead, and I never want to hear from you again."

"But Jacks, what about the children?"

"What about them? You're just a dead president, stay that way." Jackie had hung up the phone so quietly he hadn't realized it until he heard the buzz of the dial tone in his ear.

The waiter returned with the scotch, Jack opened his eyes at the sound of the liquid hitting the glass.

Bobby sat at his desk with huge piles of manila folders stacked on every possible surface. He had just enough room to open a folder and maneuver his pen around.

Kenny O'Donnell entered the office and closed the door. He came in, looked around and tried to spot Bobby.

"Who is it?" Bobby's muffled voice came from behind the piles.

Kenny stepped around papers scattered on the floor and came to a halt at the side of the huge desk. Bobby glanced at the wing tip and looked up to see who it belonged to.

"Hey Kenny, what are you doing here? Doesn't Johnson have something to keep you busy?"

"That's why I'm here. I had the most peculiar conversation with Lady Bird earlier." Kenny leaned down to pick up a folder.

Bobby put his hand out in front of him, "Don't touch anything. This is a well-organized operation and you could very well ruin my system."

Kenny chuckled and left the folder where it was. "So I was going to tell you..."

"Lunch? Yes, I'd love it. Let's meet in an hour at the Hound's Tooth." Bobby continued working but Kenny took his cue.

"Yes, see you then." Kenny left the office with a careful step.

Chapter 16

Sam Giancana stood looking out of a massive glass window at the beautiful countryside as he waited for his boss to join him.

The powerful frame of the man swept into the room as he demanded, "What the hell are you doing here? Do you understand how dangerous it is for us to be seen together?"

"Do you think I'd be here in person if this weren't a massive problem?" Giancana held his ground.

"Hurry up then." The big man threw himself onto a leather couch and lit a Cuban cigar.

"It's Jack Ruby. He's seen Nosenko."

Frankie Sinatra, Jr. sat terrified, cold, and hungry in the back of the sedan blindfolded. The drop had been made and his captor was taking him to his father. Suddenly the car pulled to a stop and the man's voice was clear.

"I'm not taking you to the drop off point."

"What?" Frankie stuttered.

"I'm afraid that your father told someone and they'll pick me up."

"No. My father would never, ever do that. He's a man of honor. You can trust him."

"I can't. I don't want to go to jail. This wasn't even my idea. I'm taking you back to the hideout."

"The hell you are. You either let me go or I'll kill you or you'll have to kill me. One of us is going to die if I don't get back to my family."

"Look, kid, I was just supposed to drive the car. I don't want to get into trouble."

"Why not drop me off somewhere close to my house and that way you'll be able to get away clean. I've never seen your face so how could I identify you? Besides, those two goons you're working with never came back to bring you your share of the money. What if they're stiffing you?"

There was silence for a few minutes and the car slid into drive again. Frankie sat in the back seat shivering with emotion until the car stopped again. The engine was cut. He heard the driver get out of the car. Silence.

Oh God, I'm going to die. What will my mother think when they find my dead body by the road? Please Lord spare her that scene.

The passenger door opened and the captor jerked Frankie's arm toward him. "Get out, kid. End of the road."

Frankie got out and the man pushed him roughly away from the car. As he hit his knees, Frankie heard the engine turn over. The tires spun gravel over his back as the car sped away.

"So, Kenny, what is this all about?" Bobby asked as he pushed mashed potatoes around his pot roast.

"Lady Bird came to see Johnson while I was searching for a file. She seemed very distressed but he was with Warren. So I asked her to tell me the problem."

Bobby looked up, his complete attention on Kenny. "It's always something with that woman. I hope you have some interesting fact to tell me not just that she wants to replace the china in the White House." Bobby fiddled with the lid on the creamer as he frowned at Kenny.

"Oh, I think this is worth hearing, Bob, she told me that when they were on Air Force One, waiting for the casket to be loaded, Johnson had a phone call from Onassis. He said basically it was all Oswald and no one else, got it Johnson or a terrible accident will happen to you on the way to the capital."

"What? I knew it." Bobby slapped his hand down on the table so hard Kenny jumped in surprise.

"I wrote what she told me word for word. Here is the file." Kenny slid it across the table for Bobby to read.

"Son of a bitch! He had John killed." Bobby nearly turned purple as he spat the words out.

"He was in on the whole thing; but, it wasn't Johnson's decision."

"It was that Greek bastard, I know it. How in the Hell did he get Johnson under his thumb? I thought he was a big strong Texan able to deal with anything. What did an alliance with Onassis gain him?"

Kenny sat and let Bobby stew for a minute. "There's something else you should know, Bob."

"I have a feeling I don't want to know."

"Johnson has been bothering Jackie."

95

"What do you mean?" Bobby shoved his plate away from him, sat up straight and watched Kenny intently.

"He's been trying to get her to visit him. I heard him on the phone with her. He told her that Papa was going to spank her if she didn't come see him."

"Shit, that crosses a line. Why didn't she tell me?" Bobby stood up and rushed out of the restaurant.

Marilyn tapped on Jack's door early the next morning. He stumbled from the bed and crossed to the threshold.

"What?"

"It's time, Jack. Open the door."

Taking the chain off the door he turned the knob and opened it a mere crack. The hall light bored into his drunken eyes. He covered them quickly with the back of one hand as Marilyn shoved her way into the room.

"You could at least offer to take one of these boxes. Have all of your manners died with you?" Marilyn dumped the boxes on the bed and began untying the strings.

"What the hell are you doing?" Jack staggered over to the bed and flung himself across the pillows with a low moan.

Marilyn turned on the lights overhead and opened the curtains. "I already told you, Jack, it's time."

"Marilyn, it is way too early in the day for these games. Get me some coffee."

"Really?" Marilyn roughly pushed a box into his side, "Get up. Then get your own coffee. I'm not your lover, your maid, your servant or your friend. Deal with it."

She opened the boxes and pulled out the garments tucked in them. She pulled out long flowing shirts with shoe string ties instead of buttons, loose fitting pants with five buttons instead of a zipper, big belts and oversized vests in bright colors then laid them on the bed.

"I must have one hell of a hangover because all of those clothes are hideous." Jack covered his eyes again with the back of one arm.

"Hangover or no they are what you are wearing. Now for the last time: GET UP!" She'd leaned over his face, yelling the last few words.

Jack jumped and nearly collided with her face as he sat up.

"Better. Now pick your outfit and be ready to go in twenty minutes." Marilyn was nearly to the door when she tossed him one last item.

Instinctively he reached up and caught it; he opened his hand to reveal a pair of rounded wire rimmed eye glasses.

Earl Warren, chief justice sat listening to the discontented swirling talk around the room. After three solid days of crabbing about the political fiasco this commission would cause, Mr. Warren abruptly left the room and marched across the street to the Oval Office in the White House.

President Johnson looked up as his door was opened without the customary knocking. "What is the meaning of this interruption?"

"I've been listening to the whining and crying of the commission for days now and I'm sick of it. This committee is a mockery to our deceased leader, our nation, and our integrity." Warren stopped his tirade as he faced the president across the desk.

"You have been appointed, Mr. Chief Justice because it is necessary to come to the proper conclusion regarding the assassination of President John F. Kennedy. You were not appointed to come in here and tattle on the other bad children in the play room. Now go do your job." Johnson went back to the paperwork on his desk, effectively trying to end the meeting.

"Mr. President, I will not be dismissed. There is no way one shooter shot John Kennedy. The discovery of the bullet in the neck from the front has disproven that theory all together."

"What are you saying?" Johnson looked up, his eyebrows raised, and put his fingertips on the bridge of his nose.

"While reviewing the tape, the president is first jerked backward and then slumps forward. That motion was caused by two bullets being shot at nearly the same time. Also the fact that Connelly was shot proves this beyond any reasonable doubt."

"No one needs to know that." Johnson's steady gaze glared at Warren, "No one."

"What are you asking us to do?"

"I am asking you, no, I am telling you to make certain that it is worded in such a way that our national security isn't questioned. There is only one shooter. We need to make the people believe that we have captured and convicted the only shooter, Lee Harvey Oswald."

Chapter 17

Agent Latimer covered the receiver with his hand and snickered to Agent Stansel, who was sitting on the opposite side of the desk.

Latimer cleared his throat and moved his hand, "Umm, yes, Mr. President. I understand, Mr. President, but there has been no change. No sir, we have not heard from Hoover." Latimer covered the receiver again and chortled at the barrage of questions.

He put the receiver into the cradle and shook his head.

"Well, Stansel, it looks like our big Texas president isn't going to bury this bone, nope, he wants to devour it." Latimer mocked in a Texas drawl.

"No, siree, Bob, he sure isn't." Stansel chimed in and both men grinned.

"Seriously, we need to find him another juicy bone to chew on. He's beginning to wear on my nerves." Latimer shook his head.

"So, we'll toss him one." Stansel stood up and left the room.

Fidel Castro waited for Aristotle Onassis to pick up the phone. It was a person to person call and the sexy sounding Greek lady had gone to fetch Onassis for him.

"This better be good." Onassis answered.

"This is the operator, has the party you wish to speak with answered the line?"

"Yes, damn it, now get off my call." Onassis roared at the operator.

"You are now connected. Good bye." A slight clicking was heard and the two men were free to talk.

"Onassis I have some news that you may be interested in knowing." Castro began.

"Well, what the hell is it? Don't you know I'm on my yacht and there's a beautiful woman naked on the sun deck?"

"War is Hell my friend." Castro snorted.

"I'm not your friend and my patience is thin. What the hell is it?"

"Sam Giancana came to see me about Nosenko. Nosenko posed as a CIA agent to gain access to Jack Ruby. Odd thing is now Nosenko is on his way to Russia."

"Look, little man, there is nothing to worry about. Jack Ruby has no dealings with the Soviet premiere."

"I wouldn't be so sure. It seems too coincidental to me." Castro lamented.

"Don't give it another thought. We'll just wait and see what Nosenko does next. Do you have a man on him?" Onassis looked out the window to see the Greek beauty strolling by in her birthday suit, gorgeous in the afternoon sunlight, and ready for his full attention.

"No." Castro interrupted.

"Why the Hell not? Idiot! Never mind, I'll handle it myself." Onassis hung up the phone, grabbed a bottle of wine on his way out the door and promptly caught up with his lady friend.

Jack Lancer stepped out of the elevator into the main lobby scratching at his thigh. He looked around the room over the wire rimmed spectacles that felt foreign on his nose. Marilyn was not there yet. The only other person in the lobby was a dark haired, gypsy woman with gold bangles covering both slender arms.

He was getting ready to have a seat when she approached him. "Here is your hat. Did you pack everything?" she indicated the bag he was carrying.

Startled, Jack merely nodded. He took the cap from her outstretched hand. "I don't wear hats."

"You do now." Marilyn picked up her own bag and headed toward the door.

"Where are we going?" Jack raced to keep pace with her.

"The Ritz in Paris, you're going to learn how to be Jack Lancer - every day guy."

Bobby sat at his favorite diner looking through a folder on his latest battle with Hoffa. He looked up as the two men slid chairs out from under the table and sat down.

"So, what is this all about?" Bobby asked Latimer as he closed the folder and gave the two men his full attention.

"Hoover. He's a royal pain in the ass. He's certain that we know vital information regarding the Marilyn Monroe affair with JFK. He thinks there's a link that will help them figure out the true reason for the assassination." Latimer smiled as the waitress came toward them but waved her away with his hand.

"Why would he think that?" Bobby toyed with the straw holder while Latimer gave the go ahead to Stansel.

"He thinks those tapes you took from the Oval Office, Marilyn's house, and Peter Lawford's home have incriminating information that should be shared with him." Stansel tapped the table with a fork.

"Well, I haven't even listened to the damn things. When would I have had time?" Bobby took a sip of his tea then dumped another spoonful of sugar in it.

"Maybe we could get those tapes from you and listen to them. We could rig them to say whatever you want them too." Stansel suggested.

Bobby thought for a moment, "No. I won't have them leaving the house. If you want to listen to them you'll have to do it in my den. Nothing leaves, not a single shred of one of those tapes. There's no doubt that they all have something sinister on them."

"Don't worry your family secrets are safe with us." Latimer stood up. "We'll be over later this evening. I'll bring the necessary equipment."

"You do realize that there are more than a hundred reels of tapes to go through." Bobby sighed, "My wife will not be happy to have you lurking in the house for weeks."

"Hoover wants a bone and we need to throw it to him sooner rather than later. It's the best plan we could come up with. Hoover is demanding the tapes and altering them is our best bet. Besides, our presence at your house brings extra protection to your family." Stansel defended his partner.

"Agreed, I'm under such pressure and this thing is out of hand. We all know there was more than one shooter. Why Johnson is insisting on a Commission I don't understand. We need an investigation and men scouring every minuet piece of evidence not a damned committee." Bobby picked up his folder, threw some bills on the table and followed the men outside.

"Johnson and Hoover are up to something. We just need to find out what. JFK was despised by those two; they hated what your brother stood for." Latimer held out his hand to Bobby. "We'll figure it all out, just leave it to us."

Bobby shook Latimer's hand and then hailed a taxi.

Chapter 18

Marita snuck into Castro's office and closed the door silently behind her. She tiptoed over to the desk and clicked on the desk lamp with a resounding noise. She held still, waiting for footsteps, holding in her breath.

Blowing out a silent sigh of relief she carefully sat down in the huge overstuffed leather desk chair that belonged to her lover, the man she was about to betray.

Slowly, carefully she lifted the receiver and dialed the operator knowing she would be long gone before the phone bill arrived.

When the operator responded, she placed a person to person call to Russia.

A sleepy voice answered.

"This is the operator. I'm trying to place a person to person call to Eduardo."

"I am that party." Yuri Nosenko acknowledged.

"Your party is on the line." The operator clicked off.

"Marita? What is the meaning of this?"

"Castro knows you are in Russia. He's very suspicious; translated he'll kill you." Marita whispered, as she stared terrified at the large wooden door to the office making certain it was still firmly closed.

"That is unfortunate. Does he know why I'm here?"

"No. He doesn't believe you would betray him for Ruby and doesn't understand your loyalty to Russia." Marita slumped further into the chair and muffled her voice in the huge back.

"Why did you use Eduardo?" Yuri asked, still lying in the dark.

"He trusts Howard Hunt and if the operator remembers who I was calling he won't suspect that I called you."

"Very good. Thank you. I owe you Marita."

"Yes you do. I'm leaving here now. I'll be in contact when I am safe. I can't risk getting caught here." Marita hung up so quietly that Yuri only heard the buzz of a dead line in his ear.

Frank sat across the picnic table in Central Park watching Bobby play with the Styrofoam coffee cup.

"I knew that Fratianno was in on it. He and Sam Giancana are in cahoots with Roselli." Frank pounded his fist on the metal table.

"Well, we can't pin it on them because no one actually saw their faces but we can use this incident in our favor. While the 'kidnappers' are claiming they did it; we know the real reason he was taken was a warning to you to keep quiet about what Sam's involvement was in the murder of my brother."

"Yes, he all but admitted he was working with Castro and Onassis on the conspiracy plot and that Oswald was a dupe. He did say there were at least two men shooting at the motorcade. One that hit Connelly and the president," Frank choked up at the mention of John, swallowed hard, "He laughed when I called him a two-bit hood."

Bobby nodded and stirred his coffee with the little plastic stick.

"I understand it's a warning for me, but what does that mean for the true shooter and how do we find out who killed John?" Frank met Bobby's gaze.

"I'll handle it, Frank. You've done enough and you've confirmed suspicions I already had." Bobby visibly softened when he saw the hurt look in Frank's eyes, "Look, from one father to another, I am relieved that Frankie, Jr. is home safe. You and the family need to heal and get on with life. Let me take care of this. Promise me you will keep your nose clean."

Bobby stood up and extended his hand to Frank. After a moment, Frank stood and firmly took Bobby's hand, in reluctant agreement. Bobby walked away leaving a bemused Sinatra watching him go.

John sat across from Marilyn in the taxi in Paris. She sat next to the window, staring out at the passing scenery, as he watched her. She was still not speaking to him. The silence loomed like a huge gray ghostly hand pushing him away.

"Okay, enough." John barked. "You can't spend the entire trip not talking to me. We've got a job to do, according to you and Bobby, so let's get this out and over."

Marilyn glared at him.

"Fine, I'll do the talking." John crossed his arms over his chest for a moment, then relaxed. He got a cigarette out and played with it as he shifted his feet. "Jackie doesn't want me. I called her on Thanksgiving. I miss the children and my family."

Marilyn watched the tortured expression on his face. "Oh God, you didn't call her. Even I didn't do that. You idiot."

"Yes, a true idiot."

"What did she say? Do? How did she act?"

"She didn't believe me at first but I convinced her it was really me. Her words hurt more than any bullet or knife ever could. She was horrible."

Marilyn watched him silently for a moment, patted his arm as he dried his tears on his sleeve.

"She said I was dead and I should stay that way. She doesn't want anything to do with me, ever. Not now or in the future. EVER."

"I'm sorry, Jack. I know how hard it is to lose everything you've worked so hard for."

"But you don't know what it's like to lose children." Jack blurted, wiping a stray tear from his eye.

"How dare you?" Marilyn spat, "I do know what it's like. My child may not have lived long enough for me to hold in my arms but I still have gone through the grief and pain of that loss."

"I'm sorry. You're right." Jack tried to pull her into his arms and comfort her but she jerked away. She refused to look at him.

Jack sat back and fidgeted with his pack of cigarettes, "I even asked Jackie to get that woman, Ruth Wallace, who had filled in for her after she had John-John, to come and stand in for her again. Give us a chance to talk."

"I remember her. Jacqueline Ruth is what they call her because she is the mirror image of your wife." Marilyn finally looked at him.

"Yes, that's the lady. But Jackie said no. She wants to live her own life and build up Camelot and the legacy that I'm going to have. I'm worth more to her dead than alive. I mean nothing to her."

"Image is important to women like Jackie." Marilyn watched him.

"I've lost everything. How do I live with this?"

"You'll get through it. I did. You're tougher than you think you are."

J. Edgar Hoover stood red faced, with his finger pointing directly at the nose of Chief Justice Warren. "I'm telling you that we need to get this god damned thing finished."

"Don't you patronize me! I have authority over this commission and you are just angry that I outrank you on this, Mr. High and Mighty Director."

The two men stood facing each other in angry silence while the rest of the committee stared with open mouthed shock.

Hoover, in a rare move, slowly sat back down. "With all due respect, President Johnson wants this wrapped up A.S.A.P. I just don't see it happening. Everyone in this room knows that there is more to the assassination than Johnson wants us to tell. WE have a moral obligation to our country to tell the truth."

"We also have an obligation to our nation to keep them safe, something you seem to have forgotten." Warren spat the words at Hoover as he sat down, "The best way to do that is to keep this information to ourselves. No conspiracy; just a lone gunman acting out a crazy fantasy."

Chapter 19

Aristotle Onassis walked proudly through the palace door in Port – au - Prince with Maria Callas on his arm. They were there celebrating her fortieth birthday with Papa Doc Duvalier, a dubious honor with political implications.

"I'm so glad you accepted my invitation. It is a rare pleasure indeed to have such a beautiful woman in my palace." Papa Doc bowed over Maria's hand and kissed the air above it.

Maria smiled, "Thank you. It's my pleasure to be in such a lovely country with you as our host."

Papa Doc laughed at her and turned to Ari. "My friend, it is good to see you again."

Aristotle hid his distaste, "And you."

"I have planned a wonderful time for us." Papa Doc eyed Maria with appreciation.

"What agenda do you have for us?" Ari firmly placed his arm around his companion as she encircled his waist.

Papa Doc chuckled, "I know how much you enjoy the black magic. I have planned a voodoo ceremony in Maria's honor."

Maria looked horrified, "Oh, Papa Doc, that is far too considerate. I could never take advantage of you in such a fashion."

"Think nothing of it, my dear. You will enjoy it. I have a few surprises in store for you."

Bobby came home early from work with a huge bouquet of roses and a box of chocolates.

Ethel came to greet him in the entry hall. Bobby sheepishly held out his offering. Ethel took the gifts and placed them on the credenza with a smile.

Ethel kissed him, "Thank you. The roses are beautiful and the chocolates divine. I know you, what's up?"

Bobby took her in his arms, "Nothing much, hon, we're just going to have a couple of agents in the den for a while."

"It must be more than that because I only get both flowers and candy when it will be a major inconvenience."

"They are going to go through the tapes from Marilyn and Peter's houses. Who knows how long it will last." Bobby kissed her passionately. "I know you won't mind, will you?"

Ethel sighed, "Of course not. Who are they?"

"Secret Service, if I tell you anymore, I'll have to kill you." Bobby laughed but Ethel crossed her arms. He knew that no nonsense looked, sighed and promptly caved, "Agents Latimer and Stansel. I promise they won't bother you too much. And besides, we could use the extra protection right now."

"Marilyn, I don't understand why you insisted on separate rooms. It would be better for our cover if we shared, don't you think?" Jack asked as he followed Marilyn down the street.

"I'm done playing games with you, Jack. I don't have any interest in you that way at all." Marilyn twisted her gold bangles around her wrist. She kept walking until they found a little outdoor café tucked in a warm corner of a plaza. She took off her wrap as she sat down allowing the warmth of the garment to cover the cold seat.

"Sit down, Jack." Marilyn arranged her flowing skirts with a flourish as she sat down on the chic little metal bistro chair.

Pouting, he sat and waited for the waitress to bring a menu. Marilyn glanced at him briefly and stifled a snicker.

Today he had chosen a pair of tight button up jeans, a long un-tucked shirt with a longer leather jacket, a hippy headband, and the glasses. His beard had grown in scraggly tufts of hair while his mustache looked more like a fuzzy peach than the manly look he was going for.

"Jack, we are going to have to find you a different disguise. This one isn't you. You can never be a hippy or a gypsy." Marilyn held up her pocket mirror for him to see. "This will never do. No one will believe it."

"What do you suggest? You're not exactly the gypsy type either. You can act the part but you don't really look it." Jack responded.

"Can you sing?" Marilyn wondered as the waiter handed them menus.

The shock showed clearly on his face, "You know I can sing you've heard me."

"I mean theatrically."

He glanced over the menu, made a choice and sat the menu on the bistro table.

"Yes, I was in the Boys choir. I was also in some productions in high school." Jack seemed a little miffed.

"Great. There is a large theatrical troupe here and we can sign with them. Can you dance?" Marilyn eyed his long legs.

"I haven't tried in a while. Bad back you know."

"Yes, well that has been corrected has it not? We'll enroll in acting and dance classes. That should get us on with an amateur troupe, at least."

"Ari, darling, I'm so glad you called." Jackie sat down on the plush sofa getting comfortable.

"I was just calling to see if you received the money I sent you." Ari inquired.

Jackie sighed disappointment, lit a cigarette and put a smile in her voice. "Yes, I sent a nice thank you note to your island. I suppose you haven't gotten it since you're gallivanting around the world." Jackie tucked her feet up on the sofa cushion.

"I'm sorry darling, but we must maintain our separate lives for appearances sake." Ari sounded truly remorseful.

"It's so difficult living in this secluded house while you get to go to grand parties and live your life. I hate being in mourning." Jackie sniffed, allowed herself a few tears then turned them off like a water spigot.

"Darling, you must persist in building your Camelot while I try to keep the French happy."

"I don't care about the stupid French or their taxes. I want to go dancing in Monaco with Grace Kelly and Prince Rainier." Jackie's hurt could be heard in her voice.

"Look darling, let's try to get you here in the next little bit. I'll send the servants away and we can have a little vacation; just you and me."

"Okay. I guess that'll be all right. You know I miss you and it's hard to read about you in the papers all the time, Ari."

"I know darling, but you really must be a good girl and continue to be the sorrow stricken widow."

"For you, I will. When are you going back to Paris?"

"We'll be heading back in a few days. Maria has that fete for Papa Doc and needs to practice. She's hired an amateur troupe to perform with her. It'll be a great farce. I've never seen anything but opera from her. She's like a giddy schoolgirl."

"I'm sure. Are you going to go ahead with the new hotel in France?"

"I don't have much of a choice politically. I need to keep both Monaco and France happy. I'll talk to you later, darling."

Chapter 20

Ava Gabor stepped off the set and onto the streets at Fox Studios heading to her trailer. As she walked, she noticed Peter Lawford heading towards another studio.

"Peter, darling, how are you?" Ava asked, as he turned toward her.

"I'm doing all right. How are you?" Peter embraced her briefly and stepped back awkwardly.

"Perfect, darling, just perfect. I heard a nasty rumor though and wondered if you could answer it." Ava flashed her most seductive smile.

"Maybe. What have you heard?" Peter swayed from side to side, nervous as a mouse about to be swallowed by a beautiful kitty.

"One of my dear friends told me that there were tapes at Marilyn's house that proved she had been murdered. Since you were such great pals with her I was hoping you would know." Ava ran a finger down his arm.

"I really couldn't say." Peter nearly stuttered.

"Darling, that's a bald faced fib. I know one when I see it." Ava stepped closer and placed her lips near his ear in a whisper, "I know there are tapes. I know you know it. I also know that you could get them for me if you would. I will make it worth your time."

Peter stepped back one giant step, "Look Ava, I really am not at liberty to say anything."

"Bobby Kennedy has them doesn't he? My friend would pay a great deal to have them. Find out what he wants for them. Anything in the world, he can just name his price." Ava blew him a kiss and walked off. She turned to find him still standing there, "Ta-ta, darling."

Yuri Nosenko was escorted into Soviet Premier Khrushchev's office.

"Thank you for seeing me on such short notice." Nosenko waited until the premier extended his hand and shook it with a hearty handshake.

"What is this about?"

"Fidel Castro is not who you think he is. He's going to withdraw the offer of help, in regards to the Americans. He feels you are losing your power to the dissidents and he will bide his time."

"That is good to know, Nosenko. What else do you have for me? Surely an encoded telegram would have sufficed for this news." Khrushchev motioned to the bottle and glasses on a tray.

Yuri shook his head, "No thanks. It would also interest you to know that he's, involved shall we say, in the Kennedy assassination. He's paid Jack Ruby off as well."

Khrushchev raised his eyebrow, "Now, that is worth coming to Russia for."

Marilyn and Jack stood next to the troupe waiting on their dance routine. Jack flirted with some of the women until Marilyn elbowed him in the ribs.

"We're supposed to be watching Maria Callas. You can get back to your whoring after the production."

"God, Marilyn you've lost all sense of fun. What has happened to you?" Jack smiled at a beautiful brunette as she danced by them, she smiled back at Jack.

"Let me just say this isn't my first 'acting' job since I left Hollywood." Marilyn leaned closer to him but kept an eye on Aristotle's lover, Maria.

"What do you mean?"

"I was in Russia this summer pretending to be Bill Walton's wife. We were invited to an art gallery opening and dinner with Khrushchev and Georgi." Marilyn picked a stray hair off of her skin tight black top.

"You're serious. But I was still 'alive' then. Why didn't I know about it?"

"You were touring Europe with Lee, supposedly. Bobby set it up with Georgi. He wanted me to secure the hot line; ensure it would work in order to avoid nuclear war between Russia and the U.S. You men do miraculous things in politics; however, a sweet, beautiful woman will melt even the hardest heart."

"That is true. Good lord, you met Khrushchev? That must have been awful for you." Jack shook his head, "How did that go?"

"He loved me, of course and I made him believe I adored him. Acting lessons paid off well in that instance. But you have to remember that it's the height of the 'smother foreign guests in our embrace' campaign he has going."

"Oh yes, Stalin." Jack smiled his understanding.

"Yes. They're still trying to undo the damage of Stalin and that so-called secret speech he read back in '56. I turned on the charm full force. I flattered him just enough for him to trust me."

"Now that I think about it, I'm not surprised at all. Good move on Bobby's part."

"It was. Bill was more than a little in love with me when my vacation was over and I went back home. He said I reminded him of Marilyn Monroe and he'd always thought she was simply gorgeous. Of course, I know that is just a sweet way of saying 'I want in your panties'."

The veteran troupe finished the last strain of the dance and returned to the wings of the stage.

Marilyn nodded to Jack, "We're up." She took her place on the stage.

Jack took his place next to her, "You must finish telling me of your adventures later."

The music started in on a lively tune with complicated dance steps. Marilyn whirled by him with a quick wink, "You got it. The best part is coming up."

Chapter 21

Papa Doc led Aristotle Onassis to the secret voodoo ceremony near the shores of his palace. The meeting place was hidden in a well secluded cove. Several others were gathered around a low fire as the two men approached.

"I'm sorry that the lovely Maria is feeling so poorly tonight. Are you sure she doesn't want me to examine her?"

"No thank you, it's merely a woman problem." Ari looked a little uncomfortable with the subject but Papa Doc just laughed.

"Perhaps it was too much to show her Philogenes' head." Papa Doc smiled broadly revealing very white teeth against the blackened skin of his voodoo make-up. "At least I had the rest of the bastard buried."

"Yes, not many people keep those kinds of ...souvenirs."

"True, however most men aren't fool enough to cross me as he did; an example that keeps the rest of them in line."

"I should imagine it would." Aristotle looked around the assembled group.

The men bowed low as Papa Doc, in full priest costume, stood near the fire. He motioned for them to stand erect. They looked curiously at Onassis but no one commented.

Aristotle stood where he was as the introduction part of the ceremony began in a chanting sing-song pitch. All the faces were decorated with white paint with various signs that only the voodoo participants understood.

The singing became more vocal as low moans were uttered from the throats of some of the men. Aristotle looked around while the hair on the back of his neck began to stand up.

Waving his hands in wild abandon, Papa Doc danced and wove around the fire for several minutes. All of a sudden, he placed his hands in the air as a deafening silence roared about them. The wind picked up and the fire flickered wildly.

"As you know our friend and confidante, Aristotle Onassis is here to have us cast another spell on our arch enemies in America. Our most recent spell has left the president dead and we are most grateful for the favor Met Kalfu."

Murmurs were heard all around until Aristotle spoke up, "Yes, we are indeed grateful but it was the shot of a gun that killed the president not a voodoo spell."

An astonished gasp escaped everyone except Papa Doc, who shook his finger in admonition at Aristotle and stared into his eyes. The force of an evil presence caused Aristotle to glance away.

"I and I alone," Papa Doc insisted, "will take credit for the demise of the hated John Kennedy. As the priest and right hand man of Jesus Christ I have willed it so."

Papa Doc's eyes shown red in the firelight as Aristotle bowed his grudging respect for the voodoo priest. "It is as you say." Onassis agreed.

"Now we are in need of another such demise from the Kennedy clan, Robert Kennedy must not live."

A vial of dirt, some hair, and an empty vial were produced and handed to Papa Doc.

"With this vial of dirt we will return Robert Kennedy to the dust he was formed in." Papa Doc dumped the dirt on the fire and took the hair from his assistant.

"With this tuft of hair from Robert Kennedy we will be certain to only harm the one we have hexed." He dropped the hair on the fire which created a slight sizzle and an acrid smell. The empty vial was passed to the priest.

"With this, the air that he breathes, we shall suck the very life out of his lungs." He dropped the vial in the fire. "As I am one with the Loa, I ask that my request be granted. Met Kalfu hear me and award your faithful...." As Papa doc uttered these last words, the assembled men began writhing on the ground while Aristotle watched in disbelief.

"Now we have proclaimed this spell and to its extent and purposes we have fashioned this doll to commemorate the occasion. Let us keep silent on this ritual and keep it amongst the brethren."

As the ceremony came to a close, Papa Doc handed Ari the finished voodoo doll of Robert Kennedy. Then Papa Doc led the way back to the palace in a reverent silence.

Maria Callas had been awaiting the return of Aristotle to their bedroom. One look at his face and she rushed into his arms. "There, there darling was it that bad?"

Ari held up the voodoo doll of Bobby Kennedy then tossed it on the bed. "I know Kennedy has one of those hated thing for me because Jackie told me so. I doubt seriously that he was at the ceremony where his doll for me was created. I truly believe that Papa Doc would not dare exceed the bounds of reasonable treachery with me. But lord that man is terrifying."

Peter waited for the ringing phone line to be answered. "Hello? Bobby? Oh, thank God."

"What's the matter now?" Bobby sighed.

"Ava Gabor caught up with me yesterday and she had some pretty wild things to say. She knows you have all of the tapes and she wants you to give them to her for her 'friend'. I'm to tell you and get them from you." Peter let out a long breath.

"Slow down Pete, you're barely making any sense at all. So she knows about the tapes. Who's her friend?" Bobby sat on the edge of the coffee table and lit a cigarette.

"She didn't say who her friend was but this friend will apparently give you anything you want. Just name your price, that's what she said."

"Tell her that I don't do business that way. I must know who the friend is before I'd be willing to do anything at all. I'm not going to give her the tapes but this friend may be a lead to who killed John." Bobby blew out some smoke rings.

"I thought that Oswald killed John."

"Yes, he did pull one of the triggers, but there was another shooter, maybe more. We need to find out who was really behind this. I'm absolutely certain that there was a conspiracy and I mean to find out from which country and who was the principal beneficiary, Pete."

"So this is far from over."

"Find out who that friend is. I'll let Stansel and Latimer know of this."

Marilyn wiped her face with a cool rag then turned back to the troupe. Maria was coming towards her with a determined look.

"Uh oh," Marilyn pointed Jack in Maria's direction.

"Woman on a mission," Jack laughed, "I wonder what she wants."

"It can't be good." Marilyn smiled tight lipped as Maria stepped up to her. "Hello Mme. Callas."

"Norma. Jack. I've been watching you and I wanted to ask you something, Norma." Maria waited for Jack to disappear.

"I'll wait outside." Jack threw his damp rag on the back of a chair and hustled off of the stage calling out to the cute brunette.

"Let's find a seat." Maria sat in a folding chair and motioned Marilyn into one across from her.

"You have the look of a star. You're not the kind of person to take back stage when you could be in the lime light. Why are you here?" Maria asked pointedly.

"Jack. He fancies the stage but hasn't ever really done anything with it. You know how it is." Marilyn shrugged, "a woman will do anything for the man she loves." Marilyn managed to look dewy eyed and softened her features to reflect the statement.

"He is charming and has a way about him. I just could have sworn that we've met before." Maria tapped a long painted finger nail on her chin.

"You and Jack? Oh, you would remember if you had met him, he's a wolf."

"Not Jack. You. I could have sworn we've met before."

Marilyn laughed, "Now honey, where would an Iowa farm girl have met such an elegant woman as yourself before?"

Maria laughed as well, "I like you, Norma. How about a song in my show? We could do a duet together. There's a jazzy little number from an American film that I just love. It's called 'Diamonds Are a Girl's Best Friend'. I can sing Jane Russell's part."

"Sounds like fun to me and I've always admired that musical." Marilyn grinned to herself, "I practically know all of the lines."

Chapter 22

Agent Latimer had just finished listening to the reels of tapes and sorting them into useable piles when Agent Stansel returned from a coffee and donut run.

"What do you have?" Stansel handed Latimer the Styrofoam coffee cup.

"Well, there are several pieces that allude to something but don't really say anything. We can make about eight reels with that." Latimer took a sip, "Thanks. I really needed that."

"What new bone are we throwing Hoover?" Stansel asked as he lowered himself to the floor next to Latimer.

"Well, I think he would love to know that Castro and Khrushchev wanted to book end the United States for a nuclear war. Perhaps that will throw him off the scent."

"But the Kennedy's already knew that." Stansel argued.

"They knew it but Hoover didn't know they knew. So we aren't giving him anything at all."

"Great, now that Hoover is taken care of what about Johnson?" Stansel asked.

"Let's tell Johnson about John F. Kennedy's other women and that Marilyn wasn't any different than any other of his numerous mistresses."

"You mean like Mary Meyer?"

"Yes, just like her."

Fidel Castro went through his desk looking for the 'secret' file.

"Damn you!" He tossed the files onto the pile on his desk then opened another drawer.

His anger over finding Marita gone had grown in the last five minutes as the vital file remained missing. "Marita you back stabbing bitch, you better hope I never find you!"

Aristotle picked up the telegram, slit open the envelope and read it over slowly; a smile grew on his face for a moment but disappeared as he read the last lines.

> Nosenko in Russia. Stop. Met with Khrushchev.
> Stop. Seen with Marita in Red Square. Stop.

Jackie and her sister Lee walked down the street in Georgetown on her way to pick Caroline up from school. Jackie held John-John by the hand as they strolled along. The press was following them and a private conversation was impossible.

As they rounded the corner a familiar car sat outside the school. Jackie walked up to the passenger window and knocked. Its electric motor hummed as the window smoothly slid down. Peeking inside, Jackie saw Bobby. He had piles of file folders stacked on the seat beside him.

"Hi Jacks, just wanted to see how you were doing today." Bobby smiled as he opened the door for John Jr. to get in with him.

"We are fine, thanks Bob. I'd like to do a little shopping today. Would you mind taking the children home for me? The maid will take care of them while I'm gone." Jackie lifted her sunglasses up to the top of her head, pulling her hair back as she did so.

"Sure, no problem at all, Jacks. You know I love spending time with them. Just wait until Caroline comes out and I'll escort them home with a slight detour to the soda fountain."

"So how are Ethel and the children?" Lee stepped up to the car door and poked her nose in.

"All are doing well. We've got a couple of FBI agents hanging around the house so I'm steering clear as much as possible."

"Keep me out of your politics, Bobby," Jackie put her sunglasses back on the bridge of her nose, as she pushed Lee out of her way, "I've got enough on my plate right now."

"Money again?"

"Always, you'd think there would be plenty." Jackie watched as Lee shook her head.

"Here let me help." Bobby took out his wallet and handed her several one hundred dollar bills.

Marita lurked around the corner from the café where she was to meet Nosenko. He was late for their meeting and she jumped at every sound behind her.

Nosenko entered the café at last and took a seat in the back booth. Marita followed him in a few moments later.

Marita took out a well battered brown envelope and handed it to Nosenko. "Here is the evidence you wanted. Castro is playing Khrushchev for a fool. Castro and Onassis are funding the dissidents that are trying to overthrow our Soviet Premier."

"I knew it." Nosenko put the envelope in his jacket pocket. "Thanks Marita. What are you going to do now?"

"I'll be moving away. I want out of all of this nasty business. This is my last spying job. I want to raise a family and be normal."

"I'll be defecting myself. This is risky information that I'm passing on and there will be a price on my head now."

"Bobby? Thank God." Teddy rushed up to his brother as they entered the White House grounds.

"What's the matter?" Bobby turned and gave his brother a quick hug. "Let's walk in the park."

They crossed the street and walked around the fountain in the center of the park.

"Are you going to tell me?" Bobby asked after they had been walking for about five minutes.

"It's another death threat. What has the Warren Commission uncovered this time?" Teddy handed Bobby the note.

"I don't know but I'll find out." Bobby gave a tight lipped smile to Teddy. "Don't worry about it."

Hoover sat at his desk going over the files that Earl Warren had just delivered to him. Thousands of pages of testimony and discussion boiled down to little useable information. He stood up to look out the window for a brief break just as two men entered his office.

"Mr. Hoover, please forgive this interruption. Your aide let us come on in." Agent Stansel stepped forward to shake Hoover's hand.

"I'm Agent Stansel and this is my partner Agent Latimer."

Hoover ignored the hand and sat back down at his desk.

"What are two Secret Service men doing in here? I hate all that you represent."

Agent Latimer stepped up to the desk and leaned over it, "The feeling is returned; don't you doubt that for a minute. But we have something you want and you have something we want. Let's say we talk about this like civilized people and come to an agreement."

"What could you possibly have that I would want?" Hoover stood back up to try to regain his advantage but Latimer was clearly taller, broader and manlier.

"I don't believe that we have been offered a seat, which is, of course the civilized and customary thing to do." Latimer didn't back down.

"Gentlemen, this isn't a social visit so the conventions won't stand here." Hoover picked at the holster where his gun was resting comfortably.

"In that case, we'll be on our way with these tapes Mr. Kennedy sent over for you."

Chapter 23

Jack lounged in a chair beside the indoor pool at the Ritz drinking brandy. Marilyn frolicked in the water with a few pasty looking French men but she didn't seem to mind with all the attention they were giving her.

After a couple of minutes, she excused herself and climbed seductively up the pool steps to the wet cement, the sultry actress was back.

A young man rushed to her side with a towel. She laughed as he draped it over her shoulders, kissed his cheek in a playful gesture and headed for Jack as she waved her fingers over her shoulder at the pouting fellow.

"Okay playtime is over. You are supposed to tell me what happened with Khrushchev."

Marilyn laughed as she stood over him dripping on his bare legs and feet.

"I can't believe that you were with him. I'm impressed." Jack smiled and took a sip of his brandy.

"Sure you are." Marilyn sat down, pulled off her swim cap and fluffed her hair with her fingers. She towel dried her legs, then stretched out on the chaise lounge and looked for the waiter.

"No, really I am. He is difficult to understand when he speaks English and he is rather sullen."

"Oh, he wasn't that night I can assure you. First we went to the restaurant where we had a full five course meal. He was laughing and joking, hanging on my every word. Then over to the opening of an art gallery, I can't remember the name of it. The art was impressionist but I knew he wasn't impressed with it."

"Doesn't he understand about art?" Jack asked, intrigued.

"Seriously, I don't think he does. You know art has just begun to make its way into Russia and he was thinking along the oil painting lines." Marilyn ordered an orange juice and champagne from the waiter.

"No, really, like scenery and grandmas?" Jack snorted into his brandy glass.

"Yep. His words were, 'A donkey could smear better art with its tail.' That wasn't the best one though. He later proclaimed the entire exhibit 'dog shit'." Marilyn laughed at the memory, "He was so furious that he had been dragged out to this 'art gallery' and to top it off he was supposed to approve of it."

"Oh, that must have been something. What did Bill say to it all or Georgi?" Jack sat up and leaned forward.

"Bill told me later that he thought it was funny that a Soviet was judging art so harshly. 'Just look at Red Square' he told me, 'they call that art'."

"What else did Bill tell you?" Jack looked serious.

"He told me that Khrushchev moved the nuclear silos out of Cuba without Castro's approval. Some people already knew that. You may have known. Apparently the potential nuclear war and what I had heard about it put me at risk with the Cubans."

"Is that another reason you wanted to talk to me? Is that why you were so adamant?" Jack reached over and took her hand in his.

Marilyn gently pulled it back to her lap, effectively releasing his hold, "Partly, I wanted to save you and I knew that there would be an attempt on your life soon. I convinced Bobby to help me figure out when they would have the best opportunity."

"Oh sweet mother of Jesus, that must have been hard for you. No wonder Bobby was so nervous. Always jumpy when I went against his advice."

"Yes, I was so grateful when I discovered you weren't the one actually assassinated but I feel horrible for that poor man who was." Marilyn's screwdriver arrived and she took a sip.

"Well, we must get to the bottom of this to keep my brothers and the U.S. safe."

Peter caught up to Ava Gabor as she was getting into her car. "Ava, do you have a minute?"

"For you, darling, but of course," Ava took the keys out of the door lock and dangled them around her fingers.

"I spoke to Bobby and he said he would be willing to help you out if you would do one thing for him first."

Ava smiled at the news. "Excellent, darling, what is it?"

"He wants to know who your friend is."

Ava's smile faded along with her pallor. "I'm not at liberty to say. Let me talk to my friend and we'll catch up later."

"I guess it's obvious that your friend is a man." Peter joked to lighten the mood.

"Aren't they all, darling?"

Ava opened the car door and got in, started the engine and sped away. Peter stood there for a moment scratching his head.

February 5, 1964

Aristotle Onassis paced furiously around the room; he was trying to hold his Greek temper in check while he waited for Prince Rainier to explain himself.

"I know we had a tentative agreement on the hotels and villas that you want to build in France as a monopoly but the French won't allow that. I'm going to have to side with them in order to secure my financial future." Prince Rainier smiled apologetically.

Aristotle stopped pacing and stood before the prince, "We've known each other a long damn time. Hell, I'm a business man first and foremost but I must tell you that it is ill-advised to cross me. An agreement is just that, a god damned agreement. I don't want to have an issue with Monaco and pull down your tourist industry. You know I can do it."

"You will do as you please at any rate; however, I have made some calls for you in Italy. Perhaps your hotels and villas would be better suited for their economy. They are willing to give you what you want." Prince Rainier stood up, signaling an end to the meeting.

"Italy? Yes, that would do. I'll take Italy." Aristotle shook hands with the prince to seal the deal. "That will teach de'Gaulle to try and circumvent me."

Chapter 24

Howard Hunt sat patiently watching the birds peck at the bread he had dropped from his sandwich. The wide open park was an excellent place to meet. Many lovers sat on blankets in Central Park and nannies strolled by with infants in carriages. It was a normal day in the life of average New Yorkers.

Marita, dressed in jeans, a free flowing shirt and a long multi-colored crocheted sweater with a pair of large rimmed sunglasses, approached the bench where Howard sat.

"May I sit here?" She asked in a typical southern drawl without a trace of her Cuban accent.

"Be my guest."

"Thank you." She seated herself and crossed her lean ankles together. "Beautiful day isn't it?"

"It is."

"It's not such a lovely day in Russia."

"Why not?" Howard continued to stare at the birds flocking around his discarded sandwich.

"There is a solid backing for those who want Khrushchev out."

"Is it infidelity that keeps this movement going?" Howard asked without looking at her.

"Indeed it is so. But there is other help as well."

He said nothing, watching the children run at the birds until they took flight.

"A tycoon has hit the Greek coast." Marita stood. "I bid you a good day, sir."

Agents Latimer and Stansel sat at the café waiting on Bobby Kennedy to make an appearance. He was a regular here and the odds of him coming in seemed particularly high since the special of the day was Kennedy's favorite on the menu, lasagna.

At three minutes after noon the duo was rewarded with the site of Robert Kennedy walking in with Kenny O'Donnell.

"Mr. Kennedy," Latimer approached the men, "would you join us for lunch?"

"Of course, we'd be delighted." Bobby followed Latimer back to the table with Kenny trailing behind.

"Can we talk openly?" Stansel asked as Kenny sat down at the table.

"Absolutely, Kenny these are Agents Stansel and Latimer. They've been helping with the assassination."

Introductions were made, meals ordered and iced tea delivered amid small talk from the men waiting for the waitress to disappear for a few minutes.

"After going over thousands of hours of tapes we have discovered something of high interest. It could be our nugget for Hoover." Agent Stansel stirred sugar in his tea.

"Well since he didn't even talk with you boys last time you met what makes you think he'll want to next time?" Bobby laughed and broke a bread stick in half.

"Oh, he will now. We've got something he wants."

"I'll try to believe you." Bobby dipped the bread in marinara sauce then took a bite.

"It's regarding you and JFK. It was at Peter Lawford's house. You were discussing Khrushchev and whether or not to give him Turkey." Latimer informed them.

"Oh, that is not a nugget for Hoover. He must never know about that. Never." Kennedy's face was pinched.

"Why not?" Stansel asked, "Isn't it in the best interest of the public to know?"

"No. Most definitely not!" Kennedy nearly choked on the bread he had just chewed up. "Those Jupiter missiles were old and needed to be removed so we decided to offer them to Khrushchev as sort of a peace keeping operative."

"If you wanted to keep peace why give the old missiles from Turkey? What significance is there to that?" Stansel leaned forward to hear the response.

"They weren't just any missiles, they were nukes."

Ava Gabor waited for Peter outside the studio. She smiled at her fellow actors as they filed past after a long day of filming. Peter came out, and she quickly fell into step beside him.

"He doesn't want his name revealed but he is willing to meet him via proxy to talk about the tapes. He is very eager to get them from Kennedy."

"I'll see what I can set up. Bobby is a very busy man." Peter hedged.

"Darling, so is my friend, but I think they each have something the other one wants."

Pat hugged Ethel as they both reached the diner at the same time, "Hey stranger, how is everyone in your 'noisy brood'?"

Ethel laughed, "When you say it Pat, the sting isn't there. Why is it that when Jackie said it, it hurt like hell?"

Pat hugged her sister-in-law, "Because, I care for you and you are a sensitive, wonderful mom who loves her children. You're not the cold ice queen that Jackie is."

"Thanks, it really makes me feel better." Ethel signaled a table for two as the hostess appeared.

They followed the woman to a secluded booth and sat down after removing their coats.

"Just tea for me," Ethel informed the waitress.

"Me too."

"Why aren't you eating?" Pat asked.

"I'm trying to retain my girlish figure. I don't want to be frumpy." Ethel giggled.

"You know Mom, she's such a lark." Pat shook her head and squeezed the lemon into the hot tea cup.

"Yes, I do. She's been very quiet since John's death."

"It's been hard on all of us. Poor mother, I don't know what it'd be like to have to deal with the loss of your favorite son."

Ethel added some honey to her tea cup and blew on the rim, "I thought Bobby was her favorite."

They both grinned for a moment then sipped tea.

"I wonder what Jackie is doing for money. It seems she never has enough of it." Pat leaned back in the booth and watched as the crowd strolled by on the street outside.

"I know Bobby has given her money. There is also a rumor that Aristotle Onassis is still courting her. Do you think it could be true?" Ethel wondered.

"She's been too public about some things and way too secretive about others. It's possible Onassis is filling her check book too." Pat tapped her spoon on the saucer, like a drummer, to the beat of the music on the jukebox.

"Poor Jackie, she is so messed up." Ethel sipped her tea, "This far-fetched dream of Camelot, for example, makes it seem they had it all together. Everyone in the family knows they were anything but a loving couple. Bobby told me John's presidency was losing its grip on the Vietnam conflict and Russia was all but a lost cause. John didn't know what he was going to do to salvage the rest of his term."

Pat nodded. "Mom thought the world of him but the truth is he was just charming and daring. He didn't know much about anything except women."

"We really shouldn't speak ill of the dead."

"True, but he was my brother and I knew him all too well. He was what he was. I loved him dearly and I always will; flaws and all." Pat wiped at a tear. "Enough of that. Do you want to hear what Mom has done lately?"

Chapter 25

Marilyn sipped champagne with Maria Callas at the bistro around the corner from the rehearsal hall. Maria was already getting tipsy.

"You know, Ari is an excellent lover. I have never been so satisfied." Maria nearly purred, then sipped more champagne.

"Really? I would never have believed that."

"Oh yes, he is very considerate of a woman's needs. Of course, it doesn't hurt that he fancies himself one." Maria giggled.

"One what?" Marilyn's eyes widened as realization dawned.

"You are silly. He loves to dress up as 'Arianna' and go out on the town." Maria snorted her laughter, "He makes one ugly woman." She downed her drink and poured another glass for herself. She held up the bottle but Marilyn shook her head 'no'. Maria sat the bottle down and picked up her glass again.

"I bet that's true. Does he really do that?" Marilyn raised her eyebrows.

"Yes and he has a tendency to beat me too. I use the same make-up to cover my bruises as I use to cover his face."

"I've heard that he has a brutal temper but why would you stay with him?"

"Yes, his temper is horrible but Ari says, 'all Greek men beat their women. He who beats well, loves well'."

Ethel grinned at Pat, "As long as it's funny."

"You know it is. Poor Mom, she's just not who she used to be." Pat sipped her tea and smiled over the tea cup, "So we were in Tiffany's shopping for diamonds. Now mother insisted that she needed a crown. Her tiara was all right but she needed a nice diamond crown to show off to her guests."

Ethel nearly choked on her tea, "What guests?"

"That is exactly the question I asked and she replied, 'Why the King and Queen are staying with us.' What? I couldn't imagine that they would ever stay with Mom and Dad but stranger things have happened."

"Don't leave me hanging, Pat, who were they?" Ethel leaned forward in anticipation.

"Are you ready for this? Frances and Kingston Queen. Mom thought they were royalty from France."

Ethel snorted, promptly covered her mouth with her hand and laughed out loud. "No! Who were they?"

"Just ordinary business associates of Dad's here from California to sign some contracts."

Johnson picked up the phone for the White House Press Secretary, "Pierre, why are you calling me?"

"Mr. President, with all due respect Mr. Kennedy wants you to, quote, leave Jackie the hell alone, unquote."

Marilyn opened another bottle of champagne and poured a sizeable amount out for Maria.

"Darling, I've really had enough." Maria put out a hand in mock protest.

"Oh, but I hate to waste it now that it's opened." Marilyn put the glass in Maria's hand.

Maria took it and sipped a little. "You know, I know all kinds of dirty little secrets about Ari."

"Really? Like bedroom talk?"

"Yes, that, but I was really meaning political talk."

"Please go on, I love gossip." Marilyn leaned forward with interest.

"I also know it was Ari who needed Marilyn Monroe out of the way. She knew too much and it scared the daylights out of him." Maria leaned back in her chair.

Marilyn kept her shock to herself and waited for Maria to continue her story.

"Apparently, Ari wanted her to marry one of his rich dictators so that he could gain influence in America. You know his reputation isn't the best there." Maria sipped some more champagne.

"That is true but how could Marilyn Monroe help his reputation?"

"Well, she had access to simply everyone who was anyone. So he thought she could bring his friends into her circle and they would introduce him later into the ripple of friends. But then she wouldn't play along. At one point he even asked her to marry him."

"Oh, she would never have married someone that much older than she was."

Maria looked up sharply, "How would you know that?"

"Why because...she just looked like she was a woman who needed a real hearty man, someone who would be able to keep up with her." Marilyn nearly stuttered over the words.

"Oh, I see what you mean." Maria looked into her nearly empty glass. Marilyn tipped the bottle to refill Maria's drink, inwardly sighing in relief.

Maria continued, "He has some shady friends and Marilyn refused to get involved with the likes of Castro and his regime. I believe her main concern was the Soviets, even though it is tough to trace his ties with them, she knew. He was entirely too open with her. He is like that when he is wooing a woman, ignorant man." Maria nearly spat the next words at Marilyn. "That dumb blonde bimbo was anything but stupid."

"Really, so what did she know that got her killed?" Marilyn prodded.

Chapter 26

Yuri Nosenko stood in the American Embassy in Russia waiting to speak to Bill Walton.

"Mr. Nosenko," Bill stepped up to him with an outstretched hand.

The two men shook with frigid cordiality as Yuri greeted the Ambassador for the U.S. "Mr. Walton, thank you for seeing me without an appointment.

Bill motioned for Yuri to follow, "Come into my office where we can be more comfortable. Can I offer you some coffee?"

"Thank you, no." They settled themselves into chairs and Bill waited expectantly. Yuri remained silent, twiddling his fingers together.

"So, what can I do for you Mr. Nosenko?"

"I need a huge favor; one that has to remain only between you and me." Yuri's eyes met Bill's in a plea of desperation.

"I'll see if I can help you but no promises."

"This is an urgent personal matter. I need to defect from Russia immediately and I want to seek asylum in America."

Jackie Kennedy sat with her sister Lee at the kitchen table sipping tea. "So the 'Camelot' fairy tale has worked miraculously well. I have the total and complete sympathy from people all over the world. The poor distraught widow ruse is working, but I still need money."

Lee added a squeeze of lemon to her teacup and stirred, "Isn't Ari giving you enough, my American Queen?"

"He does send me a generous amount but it's not enough to keep me in the lifestyle I want to live. Besides my style and fashion sense makes me a leader among women and I don't want to disappoint my subjects. I'm excellent in letting everyone else pay my way when I go out on the town but I still need a steady fluid income."

"Really, Jacks, you are incredibly selfish."

"I know. I should work on it but I'd rather just have more money."

Maria looked around the empty bistro and leaned forward almost bumping noses with Marilyn, "Yes, I do know. That bitch knew that Castro and Ari were plotting together. Ari wanted, has always wanted, to build a shipping industry empire and Castro wants to see the U.S. and capitalism die. Working together, they both fed into the other's wicked plans."

"Doesn't seem like that's a great reason to have people killed, now does it?" Marilyn frowned and leaned away from Maria a little.

"Not on the surface, but it would have allowed Ari to own and run the largest shipping conglomerate the world has ever seen. See, Ari controls what goes into and out of Monaco and he loves that power. He is a man of many passions. It is a truth, what he feels, excuses all of his wickedness and cruelties. Therefore, he does what he wants when he wants with whom he wants." Maria gently stroked the side of her face where a faint bruise had begun showing through her make-up.

J Edgar Hoover stood at the bridge overlooking the Potomac River. A few minutes later Howard Hunt joined him.

"Sir, I have information for you regarding Russia." Howard leaned on the railing and looked towards the boats heading out to sea.

"Well, go on Hunt, I don't have all day."

"Castro is inciting riots against Khrushchev with the dissidents. He has really been stirring up the pot and it looks like he will succeed; especially with Onassis funding the riots." Hunt turned on his heel and left Hoover standing at the rail staring into space.

Bobby sighed with exasperation, "Look Peter, I don't have time to talk with some mysterious son of a bitch over these damn tapes. I really just need you to deal with it."

Peter leaned against the phone booth as he looked at the store patrons, "I'm running out of answers for Ava and she is really insistent that you talk with him."

"Tell her that if he wants to talk to me it'll have to be over a weekend. I'm too busy trying to keep the death threats at bay and dealing with this god damned Warren Commission." Bobby slammed the phone down, effectively ending the conversation.

Latimer walked into Hoover's office without knocking, Stansel followed in his wake and watched as the two men stared each other down.

"Hoover, you're going to listen this time. We have vital information on these tapes that you need and I know you have information that I need." Latimer walked up to the desk where Hoover was seated and plopped the tapes down with a loud thud in front of Hoover's nose.

"Sit," Hoover motioned to the chair beside Latimer's legs.

The CIA boys took a seat while Hoover glanced at the tapes. "So, tell me what is on these tapes."

"These were taken from Peter Lawford's home in Brentwood. They clearly explain Castro's ego mania and how Onassis is funding those riots. They also will give you an idea of how big a plot this really is. It is in Onassis' best interest to have Khrushchev overthrown so that he can build his shipping industry into the massive conglomerate that he has always dreamed of. He went after Marilyn Monroe at one time to help build his image of nice guy to the U.S. and he also wants to befriend our government."

"Very interesting. But most of that I have already gleaned."

"There's more but you must give us what we want." Latimer held Hoover's gaze for a tense moment.

"What do you want?" Hoover finally asked.

"You tell us about Yuri Nosenko and why he is so important for someone who is no one."

"What makes you think I know anything about a Yuri Nosenko?"

"Come on Hoover, you're full of bullshit. You have to be as furious with Onassis about this business as we are. Let's work together on this. Or are you so inept at your job that you don't know who he is and why he's important?"

Hoover sat for a moment and tapped a finger on the end of his chin. He stared at the two men with barely concealed hatred. "Fine, what do you want to know?"

Jack had just finished tying his shoes when a knock sounded on his hotel room door. He crossed the room to look out the peep hole. Marilyn stood in the hall holding a bag and shifting a tray with a coffee urn and two mugs on it.

He unlatched the lock and opened it, taking the tray from her as she slid into the room.

"It's too early for you to be up and around after the night you had. I checked with the hotel clerk and he told me you still hadn't arrived at one this morning." Jack set the tray on the little dresser and poured them both a cup of coffee.

"I'm really exhausted but it was worth it. I got what I was after." Marilyn plopped down on the bed and leaned against the headboard.

Jack handed her a cup of the strong black coffee and dug through the bag for a baguette and some butter. He placed it on a little saucer and handed it to her.

"Are you going to keep me in suspense?" Jack fixed a few of the baguettes for himself and sat on the end of the bed at her feet.

"Maria told me that Onassis wants recognition from the United States and that he will stop at nothing to get it. He apparently is well acquainted with or funding every mafia boss in a position of power worldwide." Marilyn took a sip of her coffee, and wrinkled her nose. "Could you get me some cream?"

Jack stood up as she continued, "Apparently he had the Guatemalan president assassinated in 1957 with Johnny Roselli behind the hit. The primary reason for that hit was to see if President Armas' death could be blamed on a conspiracy theory successfully."

"Oh, my dear sweet mother of Jesus, of course it could and it was," Jack sat back down on the bed, handing Marilyn the porcelain jug of cream. "That is how Onassis did it. He plotted and planned until he had an opening. Oswald was the dupe like Sanchez was in Guatemala. It all fits so nicely."

"Yes, but there's more, Jack. Lyndon Johnson is an acquaintance of Sam Giancana."

"So? You lost me." Jack crossed his ankles trying to find a more comfortable position.

"Giancana is a friend of Jack Ruby."

Chapter 27

Aristotle grinned as he helped his lady into her seat. She smiled at him coyly and let him take her wrap. She'd dressed in impeccable style this evening as she celebrated some freedom.

"My darling, thank you for coming with me tonight. I'm aware that you don't care for Maria but it would so disappoint her and Papa Doc if we hadn't come this evening." Ari kissed her palm and licked it in a seductive caress.

"Anything for you, Ari, and I'm grateful that it's a private viewing. There won't be anyone to talk about me for having a little entertainment." Jackie flashed her brilliant smile at him.

"It's good for you." Ari hung her wrap on the hanger beside his elbow and turned back to her, bowing with practiced ease, "Would you like something to drink?"

"No thank you. Just sit down beside me and let's begin our romance anew. All I want is to touch and be touched by you." She ran her fingers over the leg of his trousers.

He took his seat and then placed his arm around her shoulders. His thumb caressed her naked skin as his fingers brushed against her neck.

Jackie shivered at the delicious feeling running down her spine. She turned her face for his kiss just as the house lights dimmed and the spotlight hit the stage. They sat there wrapped in each other's arms for a moment longer then turned to listen to Maria's speech.

John stood watching back stage as his wife sat there kissing Aristotle Onassis. He jabbed Marilyn in the ribs with his elbow and grabbed her arm to give her a look. Marilyn poked her head out from around the corner and stifled a gasp.

"Oh my!"

"What the hell is she doing here?" Jack ran his fingers through his hair. "I'm going out there. I'm going to grab her and take her outside and talk some sense into her." Jack started toward the stage exit but Marilyn grabbed his arm with her forefinger and thumb, and twisted until he yelped.

"Why did you pinch me?" Jack rubbed his arm and sneered at her, "I'm going out to get my wife!"

"Oh, no you don't. I know how this moment feels and I understand that it's almost too much to bear."

"I'm going out there and you can't stop me." Jack sounded like a petulant child.

Marilyn took a firm hold on his arm and swung him around to face her, "I'll tell you right now this won't be the last time you'll encounter a family member and you'll just have to pretend it's someone else. You can never go back, Jack, never."

Jack slumped into a folding chair and covered his eyes with a huge hand.

"Five minutes everyone. Get ready." The stage manager came through calling in a loud whisper.

Marilyn crouched beside Jack and rubbed his neck gently, "Look, of all the people in the world, I know how much this hurts. But you have to suck it up and let it go. Just try to smile through the pain and remember that life is a stage and you are always going to be an actor treading the boards."

"You make a crazy kind of sense. I guess I'll be playing a role for the rest of my life." Jack sniffed a little and glanced up at her.

"Not for the rest of your life only until you find out who you want to be. You have to reinvent yourself and it's too soon to know who you are." Marilyn stood up and stretched her legs to limber them up. She gave him a brief hug and took her place with the rest of the chorus girls. Jack slowly took his own place, deep in thought.

Johnson towered above J Edgar Hoover with a menacing glare. His veins throbbed in his temples as he struggled to keep his composure. "What do you mean Latimer and Stansel have been to see you? Why in Holy Hell didn't you tell me sooner?"

Hoover recovered from his temporary shock and stood up as tall as he could, still several inches shorter than Johnson, he puffed out his chest and yelled back, "Why in the hell does it matter to you? It is my business to handle and has nothing to do with you."

"Everything in this country has to do with me as I'm the leader of it." Johnson stomped one booted foot as he turned and stormed out of the room.

Ava Gabor sat at the Brown Derby in Hollywood with Peter Lawford. Ava tapped her fingers repeatedly on her gold cigarette case while Peter actively looked elsewhere.

Bobby Kennedy strode into the diner and took a seat next to Peter, "Hey Pete."

Bobby turned to the beautiful actress across the booth from him, "Ava, good to see you."

"Dah-lin', I never truly thought you'd come to see me." Ava held out one elegant hand and Bobby stroked her fingertips.

"Okay, Ava, you are charming and lovely, but let's cut the crap. I want to know what this is all about? Why does your 'friend' want the tapes?" Bobby nodded toward Peter's tea as the waitress approached. She smiled and turned back to get it for him.

"As you know, dah-lin', he is in desperate need of these tapes you have. We all know that there are things on them that really should be kept secret. Who knows what you will do if you keep them."

"Well the point is, I do. I have them. You can tell your 'friend' that I know exactly who he is and exactly what he wants. Unless he agrees to give me what I want there is no deal." Bobby accepted the tea from the waitress and dumped a huge pile of sugar into the glass. He stirred it quickly while he watched Ava.

"Really dah-lin' what do you want from him?"

"He knows damn good and well what I want from him. He needs to leave a certain member of my family alone in particular, as well as the rest of us in general. Beyond that, no shipping docks for him."

"Bill Walton sends his regards." Nosenko stood on the bridge and looked at the four men in black suits and ties looking for all the world like ordinary business men.

"George Joannides." He held out his hand to Nosenko. The two men shook. "We'll just get in the limo and we'll take you to the safe house."

As the men closed in around Nosenko, flanking him protectively, Nosenko visibly relaxed. "Thank you. This is such a relief. The Soviet mafia is terrifying."

"We'll keep you safe. We've got a private jet waiting." George climbed in the back seat of the limo after Nosenko.

Chapter 28

Jackie sat watching as Maria Callas and company traipsed around on the stage singing songs and dancing. Papa Doc was seated in the front row center and she would smile and wiggle her fingers at him occasionally.

After the first few numbers a jazzy little song came on and the dancers pranced around the stage. Jackie gasped as she spotted a familiar form rushing in from the wings. She looked again and leaned forward in her seat. Ari tilted his head toward her.

"What is it darling? You look like you've seen a ghost."

Jackie swallowed hard and forced a smile to her strained lips, "It's nothing, nothing at all."

He pulled her gently back in her seat and placed his arm securely around her shoulders. "Are you sure?"

"Yes. I just thought I knew someone in the troupe." Jackie took a deep breath and exhaled it slowly, following Jack with her eyes. There was no mistaking the Kennedy mouth and teeth, no matter he had a goatee and long hair.

"I see what you mean. See that dazzling blonde? She looks like Marilyn Monroe. Maria said they do a number in the second half." Ari watched Marilyn with appreciation as she spun past in the arms of a very handsome young man.

Latimer handed the file to Stansel, "Check this out. The Warren Commission has concluded that Oswald was actually aiming at Connelly. Now if that were true, then who shot John F Kennedy?"

Stansel opened the file folder and skimmed through the few pages of the newest information. "Did you see this at the very end?" Stansel pointed to the place, "Johnson knows Sam Giancana and Jimmy Fratianno, the 'Weasel'."

"Aren't they largely Castro's men?" Latimer studied the page more closely.

"Yes they are. If Johnson is friendly with these goons then he knows more than he's saying about this assassination." Stansel closed the file folder and whistled low.

"Damn! It's time to have a little chat with our new president."

Papa Doc, Ari and Jackie stood waiting for Maria to finish changing and join them. Papa Doc smiled and talked about the production.

"I really enjoyed it. I'm impressed that Maria is so talented. She's very entertaining in a satire. Honestly the only thing she didn't do exceptionally well was that 'Diamonds are a girl's best friend' number." Papa Doc laughed.

"No, that little girl onstage sounded so much like the real Marilyn Monroe that I almost believed it was Marilyn." Ari wrinkled his brow in deep thought.

"Mrs. Kennedy how did you enjoy our humble performance this evening?" Papa Doc asked.

"It was refreshing. Thank you so much for the kind invitation." Jackie nearly craned her neck as the troupe began to emerge from back stage.

No sign of the man she had watched so intently or the woman who had sung with Maria, the woman who had completely upstaged the famous operatic diva. *That young lady will be a star in no time.*

"I can't believe she's gone." Bobby hung up the phone and turned to Ethel, "Jackie went 'away for the weekend'. Where the hell did she go and why didn't she tell me she was leaving?"

Ethel sighed, "Bob, she's a grown woman and she's fine. Let her have some time to grieve alone. You don't always need to be hanging from her apron strings."

"You know she doesn't cook."

"And you know what I meant. I'm seriously getting concerned that you spend way too much time with her." Ethel folded her arms across her chest and gave a little pout.

Bobby melted and pulled her into his arms, "I do it for the children. They've lost their daddy and I can help fill that role. We must all sacrifice for their well-being."

"You're right of course. It's just you're so busy all the time and you spend a great deal of your free time with Jackie and the kids." Ethel placed her head on his shoulder and enjoyed the close moment.

"It's you that I love honey, but if the roles were reversed wouldn't you want someone to come and give you a hand with our passel of brats?"

Ethel smacked him lightly on the butt as she pulled out of his arms. "Oh, you! Why do you always make me laugh?"

Bobby pulled her back into his arms and kissed her soundly. "Don't fret, honey."

Lady Bird Johnson walked impatiently up and down the hall in front of the Oval Office. Kenny O'Donnell came around the corner and suddenly slammed right into her.

"Oh, I'm so sorry." He dropped the pile of file folders he had been carrying in order to steady her. Paper floated in all directions as he grabbed her elbow. "Are you all right?"

Lady Bird tugged at her jacket and skirt then glanced nervously up at him, "Fine. Thank you."

"I hope you haven't given our last conversation any more thought. Has your mind been put at ease?" Kenny asked as he bent down to pick up the papers and files.

"On that issue, yes, but..."

"You can tell me, Mrs. Johnson, I'm here to assist you." Kenny straightened up and began sorting through the pile of papers.

"Well I overheard Lyndon talking to Fidel about someone who had fled the country."

"Our country or his?"

"His. It seems someone named Marita has stolen some 'vital information that must be returned'. Lyndon was just getting yelled at because this Marita woman has come to the U.S. and Fidel can't find her."

"I'm sure it's nothing to be concerned about, after all she's just one little woman, right?" Kenny prodded, *this is too easy.*

"No, she's more than a woman, Lyndon said Fidel had found out she's a double agent." Lady Bird, tsk-tsked, clacking her tongue on the roof of her mouth.

Kenny and Bobby sat in the coffee shop across the street from the White House.

"The only bit of good news I've had for weeks now is Hoffa's conviction of jury tampering."

Kenny just nodded and continued with the topic at hand.

"So, why is Johnson receiving phone calls at home from Fidel Castro? Why does he know Sam Giancana and the Weasel?" Kenny spread butter on the dry muffin.

"Son of a bitch. I'm betting because he was involved with this entire plot. He was never happy being Vice President and he believed we were screwing up this country. Vietnam was a major problem, Castro another concern, and Russia was too much with the Cold War." Bobby stood up abruptly and left Kenny with a half-eaten muffin and the bill.

Chapter 29

Marilyn and Jack stood outside the airport in Paris taking their luggage out of the trunk of the cab. Marilyn watched Jack sullenly give the cabbie his fare and tip then drag his suitcase to the porter.

"Jack, you have to snap out of this funk. We don't have time for you to be mooning over her."

"How can you say that? She's my wife? The mother of my children and she was kissing Onassis. ONASSIS!"

Other people who had been bustling all around them stopped to stare at him. He smiled and waved them on.

"Please, for God's sake don't call attention to us." Marilyn smiled and leaned into his arms, whispering, "Hold me you idiot."

He obeyed instantly.

"Oh, darling, that's all right. You should stop beating yourself up over something so silly. You know I'll always take care of you." She snuggled her face close against his shoulder and pinched him under his jacket. Jack immediately responded to her pointed act.

He kissed the top of her head with exaggerated tenderness, "Thank you, I don't deserve you."

Everyone who had stopped to stare moved on after that little display, reassured that everything was all right.

A few minutes later they had boarded the plane and taken their seats. Jack stared out the window with tears brimming in his eyes. Marilyn reached over patted his arm a few times then pinched him hard.

"What the hell!" Jack rubbed the red spot.

"It's my way of bringing you back to your present situation and reminding you that the past is gone. Let it go, Jack."

"How can you say that to me? I've done well for the last few months, trying to move on, getting involved in your stupid schemes and.."

"MY stupid schemes got us the information that we needed from Maria. Now we are going to go find out what Khrushchev has to say. Don't you dare call me stupid or I'll leave you stranded."

Yuri Nosenko sat in a darkened room, a blindfold tossed on the cold metal table where his elbow rested. He had only been in the United States a few hours and he had yet to determine where he was or why he was in this particular room.

The door opened suddenly, light flooded the room for a moment and then it was gone. Yuri waited for the light to click on inside the room but it didn't nor did his visitor speak.

"What's this all about?" Yuri demanded.

A sudden blind hit to the back of his head made Yuri reel forward and slam his forehead on the table. He groaned involuntarily as another strike slammed into his shoulder forcing his body sideways and tipping the chair over from the impact.

Yuri picked himself up off the floor, stunned at this attack and blindly righted the chair. He sat in it and crossed his arms. "Do you know why," Yuri spewed blood onto the table, "I'm being treated in this abysmal fashion?"

This time the blind assault landed on his right ear, he threw his hands on the table to steady himself as he waited for the next blow.

The door opened and closed. It was impossible to tell if his assailant had left the room or if someone else had come in.

Silence.

Yuri slowly placed his hand over the ear and waited for the ringing to subside. He sat still, barely breathing while every nerve in his body was fully aware and expectant.

Nothing.

Minutes passed. His muscles began to ache yet, he wouldn't allow himself to relax. *Why is this happening? Do they not understand that I wanted to be safe and protected? Is this how they treat defectors? It is still better than facing the Soviet mafia, so I will endure it. What choice do I have anyway?*

A sudden quick jab to his mid-section sent the chair backwards taking Yuri with it. His head smacked onto the cold concrete floor and as the blood trickled out of his skull, he blacked out.

Jackie sat curled up on a chaise lounge in the middle of Ari's yacht. She had a book in one hand and her favorite vintage wine in the other. Ari lay stretched out on a deck chair beside her, sleeping.

One of the servants climbed the stairs to the deck and reluctantly awakened Ari.

"Sir, there is an urgent phone call for you."

Ari opened one eye slightly, "Who the hell is ruining my nap?"

"I cannot say sir, only that it is urgent."

"Holy shit, tell them I'll call them back." Ari had opened both eyes and glared at the poor servant.

"I tried that but, they wouldn't take no for an answer. 'Very important and cannot wait', sir."

Ari got up without another word, kissed Jackie for a long moment and then followed the servant. Jackie sat with a frown between her brows for a second, shrugged and returned to her book.

"What the hell is it?" Ari barked into the receiver.

"Never take that tone with me," Papa Doc warned.

"Fine, what is so important?"

"I have been thinking about that blonde who performed the song with Maria. It was something about diamonds."

"So? This hardly seems urgent."

"Perhaps it doesn't seem that way but if this is Marilyn Monroe she will still be onto our plans and could be very dangerous to us both. Simply put, I want you to find her."

"Ok, say I do find her. What do I do with her?" Ari yawned and watched the ocean waves as they drifted on the sea.

"Take her someplace secluded and let me come visit with the bitch. Do you still have Howard Hughes holed up on your island?"

"Yes, you know I do. He's heavily guarded by the Mormon Mafia. Why?"

"It's pretty simple, Onassis, get them to guard our new friend in the same way. Something just doesn't feel right about this."

Chapter 30

President Johnson had just stepped out of the limo when Stansel and Latimer approached him, "We need a word, Mr. President."

Latimer blocked the president from leaving the protection of the car standing in the door while Stansel flashed his badge at the secret service men protecting Johnson who had jumped from the car and were now standing on the curb.

"Mr. President, we've found out the information you requested. It seems that JFK had affairs with numerous women, none of them were special. Apparently, Ms. Monroe was just one in a long line of women friends that enjoyed the honor of sleeping with a president."

Jackie sat back on the sofa, a cup of hot tea steaming in front of her while Caroline regaled her with stories of her weekend. For the moment the child was happy and animated. John Jr. sat curled next to his mother, with his head cushioned on the pillows and a model airplane spinning in childlike circles as far as his outstretched hand would allow.

It was moments like this when Jackie's mind could wonder while she responded to the children in a semi-caring state.

"Mother, did you hear me?"

"What darling?" Jackie's full attention returned to her now sober daughter who looked like she was about to cry. "Freddie said that daddy deserved to be shot." Caroline repeated.

"Oh no, honey. Never believe it, never! Your daddy was a great man." Jackie leaned forward and patted her daughter's shoulder, pulled her to her in a brief hug.

"Freddie said his daddy thought my daddy was a menace to our country. What does that mean, mommy?" Caroline rubbed the tears out of her eyes.

"He doesn't know what he's talking about, honey. Don't you worry," Jackie reached over and stroked the child's face.

"But why would Freddie say such a thing? How could he be so mean?" Caroline tried to wiggle back into her mother's embrace but Jackie had already turned to her teacup.

"Ignorance, just don't listen to him." Jackie patted the child's face with her free hand, "Run along and play with your brother. Mommy has lots of things to do now I'm home."

Jack watched Marilyn work her magic with Khrushchev while the beautiful woman beside him ran her fingers up his arm and tickled his neck with her fingernails.

Marilyn giggled and Khrushchev leaned closer to her, looking down into the valley between her breasts created by the skin tight cocktail dress she was wearing.

Jack kissed the fingers that made their way seductively onto his lip. He smiled at the stunning brunette, brought in to distract him from Marilyn's flirting with the Premier. She stood up, smiling as she grabbed his tie and encouraged him to stand with her. He stood, then put her mink stole around her shoulders and handed her the evening bag lying on the table.

Khrushchev smiled at the couple as they prepared to leave.

"Good night, all." Jack glanced around at the group of mostly drunken diplomats and politicians. "Can you find your way back to the hotel, Norma?"

"I'll make shure shee gets there." Bill Walton spoke up, his speech slurred by the liquor.

Marilyn smiled, "Oh, I think I'll be fine. I can always get a car. Good night."

George Joannides listened as Ari ranted on the other end of the receiver. He held the phone away from his ear as a turret of curses flowed from Onassis' mouth. Finally, the tirade stopped.

Joannides tentatively spoke, "All I can confirm is Nosenko has been accepted by the United States, he has defected from Russia and he is at an undisclosed location where he is being interrogated."

"Find that son-of-a-bitch and kill him!"

"No, no my friend," George tried to calm Ari down, "he could be a valuable asset to us. He could provide information, of our choosing, to the Americans."

"You better be right on this Joannides, or your head will be on the chopping block with Nosenko." Ari hung up.

As Marilyn's hotel door crashed open, she sat bolt up -right in the bed, pulled off the eye mask, and grabbed for the gun under her pillow in one fluid motion.

Two masked men erupted into the room as she slid onto the floor on the opposite side of the bed. She still groped under the pillows for the gun as the men began to close in on her, one leapt onto the bed while the other ran to block her way between the wall and the footboard.

Her fingers grasped the barrel of the gun and she pulled it out. The man on the bed noticed and gave her wrist a sharp smack forcing her fingers open while he pounced on the bed towering over her crouched figure on the floor. The gun landed on the bed in between them. She lunged for it but he stepped on her hand.

The other assailant jerked her forcefully from behind and jabbed a needle in her arm. As she slid into the black fog, Marilyn numbly shook her head, *Oh God, not again.*

Chapter 31

"Johnson, need I remind you, there are those four charges which were brought against you before Kennedy was assassinated and now they have suddenly disappeared? Would you like them to reappear?" Aristotle sounded smug on the other end of the phone.

"No, Onassis there will be no need for that."

"You will recall one of those very charges disappeared the day Kennedy was shot. I could very well inform those on the committee to reinstate those charges."

"That won't be necessary. What do you want?" Johnson sat, suddenly realization of his position hit him.

Approaching the door to his hotel, Jack noticed it wasn't shut. He stopped, pulled the gun from the waistband at the back of his pants and held it beside his leg close to the wall. He stayed near it, protecting himself, as he slowly opened the door with the pistol.

The light was on and the entire room was in shambles. His clothing and personal items were thrown about, the bedding was on the floor and the mattress, sofa and chairs had all been torn to shreds by the sharp end of a knife.

Panic assailed him as he raced down the hall to Marilyn's room. He pushed that door open with his free hand and barreled into the suite. Her room looked much like his with the exception of the discarded black eye mask and a tube of lipstick lying on the dressing table.

He searched the bathroom, finding nothing of interest in there; he returned to the bed, sat down, rubbed his still half drunken head and groaned.

"Now what?" he ran his fingers through his hair and groaned a second time, "Bobby is going to kill me."

Howard Hunt stood in the opulent office of Fidel Castro in Cuba. Castro had been ignoring him for the better part of half an hour while he chatted on the phone about his troops, or lack thereof, regrouping.

Hunt leaned over the desk, and got right in Castro's face, "I hate to interrupt your little military planning party; but what I've come here to tell you, is a matter of life or death, namely ours."

Castro hung up abruptly, "How dare you interrupt me!" He stood up, pointing at Hunt, "You insolent little bastard."

"Go ahead, threaten me, kill me, even; but it'll still be your neck in the sling once Onassis realizes that his demands aren't

met. You don't know what the problem is so he'll kill you too."
Hunt sat down, crossed his legs and took a cigar from the box.

Castro took his seat but glared at Hunt.

"First, Nosenko has defected from Russia. Everyone knows it and he's a threat to our mission." Hunt bit the end of the cigar off and spit it in the ashtray.

"How did this happen?"

"Irrelevant to our mission." Hunt waved away the protest, "Now we need to move up our timeline." Hunt puffed on the end of the cigar until it lit, "Onassis needs Khrushchev out of the way. It's time to get Bolshakov moving on the overthrow of the premier and get the dissidents in."

"How are you going to handle that?" Castro blew a few smoke rings in the air.

"Me? That is your job. I'm not the paid assassin." Hunt glanced at Castro with disdain.

"Maybe not, but once Khrushchev is overthrown; you will have to kill Bolshakov. He cannot live."

"You want me to go to Russia and kill him?"

"No, but it's what you will do."

Marilyn came awake slowly to the tingling sensation in her left leg. She swallowed the bile that threatened to explode from her throat and held her breath until the nausea passed.

She wiggled a bit in her confined space as the realization hit her she was in the trunk of a moving car. Her hands were bound behind her back, a fact which was achingly clear from the screaming muscles in her shoulders. She tried to roll into a more comfortable position but her movements were blocked by hard sharp objects on either side of her.

Frowning, Marilyn swallowed again and blinked her eyes several times. The taillight came into focus from the inside of her prison giving her a tiny flicker of light. She stared at it and tried to focus her full attention on it as the rocking and swaying of the car brought a new wave of nausea into her mouth. She gulped, desperately trying to keep from soiling herself in her own vomit.

What the hell is going on? Where is Jack? Did they kill him? She groped the objects behind her back trying to find something that would slit the rough rope holding her prisoner. Her hand slid across a jagged edge, *Damn I'm bleeding.*

She wiggled her hips down lower and moved her wrists back and forth against the broken glass until she felt a slight give in the rope. Sweating and terrified, she struggled to free her hands as the movement of the car slowed to a stop.

Chapter 32

Ethel answered the phone, "Hello?"

"This is the operator. I have a person to person call for a Mr. Robert Kennedy. Is he available?"

"Yes, hold on operator," Ethel nudged Bobby who was still sleeping beside her in the bed. "Phone for you," Ethel handed the receiver to her groggy husband. "It's the operator again. Person to person."

"This is Robert Kennedy." Bobby cleared his throat.

"Will you accept the charges from a Mr. Jack Lancer?" the heavy Soviet accented operator asked.

"Yes."

"Your party is on the line."

"Bobby, thank the sweet virgin Mary." Jack began in a rush, "They've taken her Bob, I don't know where. The rooms are torn apart and she's just gone."

"Slow down Mr. Lancer, I can't understand you." Bobby sat up straighter in his bed and flipped on the table lamp.

"Marilyn. She's gone. All that's left is her lipstick and an eye mask." Jack ran his fingers through his hair and tried to stop pacing.

"I see." Bobby sat still for a moment. Ethel sat up beside him with a worried look. He turned to her, covered the phone with his palm, "Honey, everything is fine. Can you go make me some warm milk so we can go back to sleep?"

Ethel shook her head, "I'll just leave. I know you have secrets you can't tell me but 'warm milk'? Honestly."

Ethel chuckled, patted his leg, got up and left the room.

"Now, Jack, try and calm down. What happened?"

Jack recounted what he knew, then ended in his own defense, "I was only gone a few hours."

"Well, they were definitely watching you both. They knew she'd be alone. I know who is behind this and I know how to get her back. You won't be any help to me if you go chasing after her. I need you to go talk to Georgi and tell him that the Premier is in trouble."

"But I want to save her. I've allowed this to happen. I didn't protect her." Jack sighed and sat down on the bed. He pulled a cigarette out of the carton, tapped it on the table then lit it.

"Well, you can't right now. I can get her back but only if you lay low. No one knows about you. Let's keep it that way." Bobby heard Ethel coming back up the stairs.

"What do I do?'

"I'll send you a telegram in the morning. For God's sake Jack, don't be a pussy. Pull it together and follow my instructions. We've got enough trouble without you screwing this up."

"Look who's all grown up." Jack sneered.

"Yes, and look who's all fucked up." Bobby hung up the phone and tried to smile as Ethel appeared in the doorway.

Frank Sinatra had just finished belting out his favorite tune at the Sands hotel in Las Vegas when his friends, Johnny Roselli and Jimmy Fratianno were seated in one of the plush round tables at the front of the stage.

He smiled at them and began a tender rendition of "Bewitched, Bothered and Bewildered" while the ladies in the audience leaned forward exposing cleavage for his eyes alone.

As he began the chorus for the second time, Frank's eyebrows shot up as Robert Maheu slid into the booth beside them and handed them both envelopes. The men casually slid them into pockets without missing a beat of the show. *No one would even realize what just happened even if they did see it.*

The set finished and he introduced Dean Martin. Frank came off the stage and greeted the three men as he slid beside Roselli.

"Gentlemen, it's nice to have you here tonight. To what do I owe the pleasure?" Frank nodded as the waiter plopped down drinks for them all.

"Just a little business with some entertainment mixed in. Frank, great song," Maheu took a hearty drink then lit a cigarette.

"Yes, I noticed the little bit of business." Frank nodded as the two goons patted their lined pockets.

"My boss just wanted to congratulate them for a job well done. But there is no need to talk about it. It's such a nasty business."

They sat there drinking and listening to Dean Martin, Sammy Davis Jr., and Shirley McClain making jokes and singing.

"Frankie," Shirley wiggled her finger at him, "I'm lonely, Frankie, come up here and keep me company."

The audience laughed and applauded as Frank made his way back to the stage with a smile.

Roselli, Maheu, and Fratianno started to talk freely as the alcohol loosened their tongues.

Roselli, "Thank Aristotle for us. The agreed payment would have been enough."

"He just wanted to make it clear that you should never speak of this 'incident' ever to anyone." Maheu swirled the last of his martini and then drank it down.

"Why would we do that? If we utter a single word, we'll be just as dead as the president we killed." Fratianno slapped a hand over his mouth. "Oh, you mean like that?"

"Yes." Maheu glowered at him, "That better never happen again or you'll be inexpiably missing. Understand?"

Fratianno's adam's apple bobbed up and down as he swallowed hard, "Yes."

Maheu got up and left a one-hundred-dollar bill on the table. "Enjoy the rest of your evening, gents. Remember, I'm always watching you."

April 05, 1964

Jackie sat with her mother on the couch sipping tea as John-John and Caroline played with Lincoln logs on the floor. Jackie sighed as the phone rang.

"Hello?"

"Jackie, darling girl, I wanted to call and personally invite you to the dedication of the Rose Garden at the White House for your husband. I know what this will mean to you." Lyndon's smile could be heard in his voice.

"Thank you, Mr. President it's very kind of you." Jackie made a disgusted face to her mother, who laughed silently at her.

"I trust I will see you there."

"Now Mr. President it's not nice for you to press. I've already sent back the RSVP. You'll just need to check with Lady Bird on that." Jackie tossed a Lincoln log at John Jr., he screamed in surprise. "Oh dear, the baby is crying. I must go." Jackie hung up the receiver.

John-John smiled at her as he picked up the toy his mother had tossed at him and placed it on his stack. She smiled back.

"Mother, I can't make myself spend an afternoon with that insufferable jack ass." Jackie picked her tea cup back up and sipped at it gingerly.

"But you must go. John was your husband and the family must be represented. Think how it will look to the country. Really, Jackie your selfishness surprises even me sometimes."

"Well, Mother, if you think the 'family' needs to be represented then you go. Here is the invitation." Jackie handed her the embossed card and effectively changed the subject. "Isn't it lovely how the weather is changing? I do so love the cherry blossoms, don't you?"

Chapter 33

The key turned in the trunk lock as the two men began arguing, Marilyn couldn't understand what they were talking about but they weren't focused on her. As the lock sprang the trunk lid open, she jumped up, socked the closest one in the nose with a mighty force.

"Damn it, bitch." The stunned captor held his profusely bleeding nose and yelled, "Get her."

Marilyn jumped off the fender of the car and took off as fast as her legs would carry her. She ignored the stinging needles pulsing in her blood from hours of being stuck in the same position. There was a vast ocean to her right and a large house to the left and very little in between. *An island, shit!*

The mafia man was right behind her but there was really nowhere to go. The evening light was fading slowly over the water. He stopped chasing her when she got close to the water and waited. His arms crossed over his chest and a smirk on his face.

"Fine," she said as he stood watching her. "I may not have anywhere to go but you'll have to come get me."

Marilyn planted her feet firmly in the sand and grabbed the shard of glass as tight as she dared. As he casually walked towards her, she leapt forward, slashing his cheek with the glass.

He slapped her down to the sand with one fluid unseen movement, "You fucking whore. What the hell are you doing?" He threw his palm over the bleeding wound.

The other man with the broken nose ran up to join them as Marilyn slowly got to her feet. "What the hell are you doing with me? What do you want?"

"WE don't answer the questions, you do, bitch." The man with the broken nose grabbed her arm and slapped the glass onto the beach. He turned to his companion, "How are you going to explain you got a gash from a mere woman?" He laughed for a second but stopped abruptly as the pain in his face reminded him she had gotten the better of him too.

"Same as you, lie about it."

They grabbed her under her arms and picked her up under the knees keeping her from hitting or kicking them. She laughed at them as they carried her back to the huge house.

"You aren't allowed to hurt me are you?" She mocked, "Well that's such a shame isn't it?"

The men continued to carry her without answering.

"Who sent you? Let me guess." Marilyn tilted her head toward each man and noticed the symbolic pen on their lapels. "You're part of the Mormon mafia."

The one with the broken nose gave her a startled look. "So, I'm right." Marilyn grinned, "So are you Abbott and Costello or Moe and Curly from the Three Stooges?"

They ignored the barb and carried her through the massive front doors and down the stairs to a dark basement. The big one with the gash held her firmly against his chest as the other man inserted an ancient looking key into a huge lock. Once the door was opened, he tossed her into the room and slammed the door shut, locking her in.

Maria stood naked looking in the mirror while Ari watched her brush her hair. She was a beautiful woman and she knew it. She took long slow strokes with the brush allowing her dark mane to shine and gleam in the candle light surrounding the room. She was teasing him and they both knew it.

"Darling, you know we need to talk business. Aren't you satisfied yet?' Ari sat up in the bed and lit a cigarette.

"I'm never satisfied, neither in love nor business. You should know me well enough by now." Maria turned, pulling the brush through her hair and allowing it to fall over her breasts.

"Yes, but we need to talk about the hotel chain in Italy. I want the monopoly and they've agreed. The question is how do we legalize gambling? It was so much easier in Monaco."

Maria tossed the brush down on the dresser and pulled her satin robe around her nakedness; tying it around her waist with a tight tug. "Business. It's always business with you. I doubt seriously if you talk 'business' with your American lover."

"Don't be catty Maria, it doesn't suit you." Ari tapped the ashes into a tray.

"Why do you insist on pursuing her? She's cold and aloof." Maria came over to the bed and slid in beside him. Smiling, she ran her fingers through his chest hair.

"That she is, except in bed. There she is all fire and warmth." Ari chuckled as Maria smacked her doubled up fist into his forearm. "Really, kitten, you should know you can't hurt me that way."

Maria moved over to the other side of the bed, crossed her arms and closed her eyes.

"I pursue her because she can give me what I want." Ari sat awaiting her curiosity to get her to ask. After a moment, she turned to him.

"And that is entrance into the hearts and business pockets of the Americans. You don't honestly think that they will accept you? You've brought down the wrath of their government on more than one occasion. Why would they trust you?" Maria asked.

"If I can win the trust of their beloved grieving widow, it should be reasonable that the rest of the nation will follow suit. It's a game, Maria, that's all, but you know I play to win."

Johnson sat reviewing the latest military covert operations procedures he had approved and smiled. His plan of escalating this Vietnam conflict into a war was coming together slowly but piece by piece.

His door slammed open and Sam Giancana stood in the frame.

Before Johnson could utter a word, Giancana strode quickly up to his desk, leaned over, grabbed Johnson by his tie, twisted it tight, and growled into his ear, "The

190

establishment has grown impatient with you. These little games you have set up are child's play and not acceptable. You have one month to get the military involvement moving towards war or we'll find your replacement."

Sam let go of Johnson abruptly. Johnson leaned back in his chair gasping for air. Giancana disappeared as quickly as he had arrived.

George Joannides waited until the secret service man answered the hotline. "Stop beating Nosenko. I'll be there in a few days to talk to him. Give him some decent food and let him get some fresh air. I want his brain clear for our talk."

"Yes, sir."

Chapter 34

Jack and Bill Walton sat at the Sovietskaya restaurant. They had finished dinner and were drinking vodka.

"Norma has been kidnapped and you're here to get a message to Georgi? Why aren't you going after her? She's an amazing woman." Bill slurred his words a bit but was still sober enough to be mad.

"Bobby has ordered me to stay out of it. He says he can get her back and he knows where she is."

"Who all knows that you're not dead?"

"You, Bobby, Norma and Kenny, that's it. No one else must ever know." Jack sipped his vodka, trying to stay sober.

"So what message am I passing along to Georgi?"

"Look Bill this is important, you can't get this information wrong. Are you sure you're sober enough to remember?"

"Of course, I live in Russia, we're taught to hold our liquor."

"Yes, but you're not Soviet. Maybe I should try to talk to him myself."

"He'll know you as soon as he sees you, disguise or no. There is no hiding those teeth or that chin." Bill chuckled.

"Fine, let's meet for breakfast and I'll give you the message, hopefully you'll be sober enough to remember it then." Jack stood up and tossed back the remainder of the vodka.

"You know, I'm in love with her." Bill stated as Jack froze in his tracks.

"Norma?"

"Of course, Norma. Who else? If anything happens to her, I'll just kill myself. I almost asked her to stay here with me and let me take care of her. I don't like that she's always running around spying."

"That's noble of you, Bill." Jack sat back down.

"Have you ever really loved someone Jack? You're such a playboy; I doubt it. You know, loved a woman like the world would end if she wasn't happy?" Bill knocked back the rest of his vodka, "Maybe it's just the liquor talking but I want to marry her."

"Mr. Kennedy, the telegram has been intercepted." Latimer told Bobby as they walked along the square in DC.

"Great. Let me see it."

Got the package. Stop. Island winds are blowing. Stop. Awaiting further instructions. Stop.

Bobby laughed, "This is terrific work, Latimer. Now we'll respond to them."

Latimer stood still with a pen and notepad while Bobby thought.

"Okay. 'Keep the package safe. Sending a nurse to handle feminine needs. Allow the package freedom with escort."

"You got it Mr. Kennedy. We'll send this right away."

Papa Doc Duvalier stood behind his desk, with the telephone receiver to his ear and cigar in his mouth. The ringing was finally answered on the other end.

"This is Johnson. What do you need Duvalier?"

"Why have you not reinstated the financial aid to Haiti, my beloved country, per your agreement with, let us say, our mutual friend? Don't you understand that we are the portal that you need for this Cuban conflict?"

"Contrary to what you think, Duvalier, we don't need your tiny little piece of land to handle anything. The U. S. government feels it is a waste of money to continue to fund your efforts."

"No, no, my friend, that will not do at all. You listen carefully. It is I who can help you in this struggle against communism." Duvalier's voice had taken on a harsh insistent tone.

"Really?" Johnson chuckled, "please explain that to me."

"Communism has established centers of infection. No area in the world is as vital to American security as the Caribbean. We need a massive injection of money to reset the country on its feet, and this injection can come only from our great, capable friend and neighbor the United States."

"That's a real nice speech." Johnson gritted his teeth, "You know this is not something I can unilaterally approve."

"True, but none the less, you will make it happen."

"I'll see what I can do." Johnson hung up, shivering despite himself.

Marilyn stretched and yawned as she came awake in the small basement room with a dim light coming in from a tiny window near the ceiling. She moaned as she rolled over on the army cot.

She blinked as she heard a movement a few feet away from her. She focused her eyes on a well-groomed man who sat on a metal folding chair watching her intently.

"You're very grimy, you know that don't you?" he asked.

"Yes, I should imagine I am. I've been through quite a lot, as you should know." Marilyn struggled to sit up on her elbow, her hand throbbed but someone had bandaged it.

"Why would I know anything about you?" he stared at her as she struggled to a full sitting position.

"What?"

He sighed, a long suffering sound of impatience, "Why...would...I..."

"Stop. You know what I mean. You've kidnapped me and put me in here. Why?" Marilyn let out an exasperated sigh of her own.

"I?" his eyebrows raised in surprise, "I don't even know you. Why would I do such a thing? Besides you're far too nasty for me to touch."

He stood up and leaned a little closer to her. As the light hit him fully in the face she gasped, "Howard? Why, you're Howard Hughes aren't you?"

"I once was but now, now I don't know who I am."

Chapter 35

"But Jackie, I've invited Bobby and Ethel to my party and you're not coming."

"What do you mean I'm 'not coming'?" Jackie blew out her breath and released the cigarette smoke she'd been holding in her lungs. "Lee you are inviting me and I'll be there."

"Not this time you aren't, my dear sister. You're not getting your way today Jacks. You're taking Ari from me and I'm getting my little revenge on you. What are sisters for if not to make each other miserable now and again?"

"This is bull shit. You know they are my family. Why are you being so mean?'

"Cut the theatrics. I know you don't care about this party."

"I really needed to talk to you about something serious and now I can't." Jackie sniffed and stabbed out her cigarette in the ashtray at her elbow.

"Serious?" Lee changed to a more sympathetic tone, "What's wrong?"

"Why do you care? You just want to torture me with your little parties and petty jealousy."

Khrushchev and Brezhnev stood facing each other in a heated argument. Georgi Bolshakov listened behind a closed door with his hand over his mouth.

"Seriously, you are not that naïve, Khrushchev." Leonid Brezhnev shook with rage, "I know the collective leadership should be in place by now but you are allowing this to drag on so you can keep all the power."

"What you don't understand, is that I'm not naïve, I know the dissidents want a more democratic way of life without my leadership. That is what you don't understand. I know too well that I will be out once they get their way."

"Soon, you will have to let go." Leonid stormed out of the room nearly running down Georgi in his rage. Georgi made a hasty exit down the hall keeping out of sight of the two furious men.

"Come on, Jacks, you know I care about you. Do tell me what's wrong."

It's about John." Jackie picked up her tea cup and took a small sip.

"Are you having those nightmares again?"

"No. I just sometimes believe he's still alive somewhere. Maybe it was all a mistake and it never happened."

"That's to be expected after what you've been through. The mind is trying to cope with what the eyes saw. Have you been to see Dr. Feel Good lately?"

"No, Lee you don't understand. I have this conviction that he really *is* alive somewhere. I don't know, maybe he's running around having a good time while I'm here dealing with all of this aftermath." Jackie put her tea cup down and tucked her feet up underneath her. She pulled the crocheted afghan around her legs and leaned back on the couch.

"Look honey, you really need to talk to a shrink about these thoughts. It's normal to feel like it was all just a nightmare but you and I know that we buried him a few months ago. I'm really worried about you now. Please promise you'll make an appointment and go see your shrink." Lee's voice was pleading.

"But Lee, you just can't understand this, can you? I just feel he's still here."

"I know, honey, I can't even begin to imagine what this must be like for you."

"No, like he's really still alive."

"Nosenko, I've saved your miserable life. Now do be honest with me and tell me what you know." Joannides sat across a nice wooden table from Yuri.

The beatings had stopped a few days earlier and he was beginning to heal from his wounds. Nosenko grimaced as he placed his hand on the table.

"If I didn't tell those goons who broke my arm, nose and ribs anything why should I tell you? I merely wanted protection from the Soviet mafia. I honestly just want to live a normal life in peace without fear of being hunted down and killed like a dear running in the woods." Nosenko held Joannides' gaze until Joannides looked away.

"While it is true you have kept silent despite your tortures, I have an obligation to my boss to know for a certainty you will not ever divulge what you may know." Joannides lit a cigarette and puffed it for a moment.

"All I know is I want to live my life. I'll never tell you or anyone else what I may or may not know in regards to anything or everything. I'm a man of my word. You need not worry I'll create issues for the United States or your government." Nosenko shifted in his seat to find a more comfortable position for his aching ribs.

"Let us hope that's true, Mr. Nosenko, as we'll always be watching you."

Jack and Bill Walton sat in Red Square feeding the never ending pigeons that flocked the area for crumbs dropped by the peasants and tourists.

"I told Georgi what you said about Castro and the dissidents. He already knew it. So my question is why did he already know?" Bill furrowed his brow as Jack tossed crumbs to the birds.

"Do you think he's a double agent?" Jack turned to Bill.

"I'm beginning to think our dear and trusted friend is just that." Bill got up and left Jack staring after him.

Chapter 36

Marilyn stood beside Howard Hughes watching as he tapped three times on the wooded wall. Suddenly the wall swung wide, he stepped into the room as she fell in behind him. They were standing in an old library. Marilyn's eyes widened as they crept through the musty smelling room, but she held her silence. Howard had squatted down and waddled like a duck past the huge open windows. Marilyn followed his lead and got on all fours to crawl past them.

Howard popped up as soon as the wall blocked the outside world from view. He strolled with confidence to the doorway and opened it a crack. He turned the knob with a Kleenex he got out of his pocket. He looked at her and grinned then slipped out the door and into the hallway.

Marilyn followed, *What the hell is he doing?*

After they had passed a few closed doors, he stopped, placed his ear to another door and listened. Marilyn looked up and down the hall making sure no one was watching them.

He slowly opened the door, again using a Kleenex to push the door open, using extreme care that his hand never touched the door. Marilyn smiled at his oddities.

As he slid into the room, she quickly did the same. He stood still for a moment, allowing his eyes to adjust to the dim light in the room. Marilyn watched as he expertly made his way into the center and flipped on a small light over the stove.

"The kitchen? What are we doing here?" Marilyn looked around the room and snagged an apple out of a bowl as her stomach growled.

"I'm hungry and apparently so are you." Howard glanced down at her mid-section. "I don't trust anything they bring me and never eat it. 'They' don't understand why I haven't died yet." Howard chuckled as he opened the door to the ice box and took out some cheese, ham and lettuce.

He pulled open a drawer under the counter and pulled out a loaf of bread. Snagging a couple of paper towels, he began to assemble the sandwiches while Marilyn scouted around for more fruit.

"Don't they miss the bread?" She turned to him with a handful of grapes dangling from the branch.

"No, the employees come and go as they want. The kitchen isn't staffed so no one keeps an inventory." Howard handed her a sandwich and began eating his own.

"How did you figure this out?" Marilyn bit into her sandwich with appreciation.

"They try and keep me drugged but I figured out a long time ago it's only in the food. As long as I am docile and quiet they don't question anything. If I act out of character they give me a shot. One day one of my 'keepers' asked me if I was hungry when I hadn't eaten what they brought me."

"I still don't understand." Marilyn watched him as she chewed on her sandwich.

"He thought I wasn't listening when he asked the man at the door to get me something else and drug it. But I heard. I'm not as crazy as everyone thinks I am. I just make sure to throw away what they give me." Howard smiled while brushing imaginary dust from his sleeve.

"So how long have you been here?"

"I was brought here in '58. It's my own fault really. I had Maheu hire Rector to stand in for me. People are so germy. Onassis wanted control of my fortune and laundering capabilities in Vegas and he owned Maheu. So, one day I'm whisked away to this island paradise."

"And you're okay with it? Have you tried to escape?" Marilyn sounded amazed.

"I've never wanted to escape, why should I? I'd love to fly again but I like the peacefulness, the sound of the ocean waves and the goons don't bother me as long as I'm in my room."

"So they don't have any idea you wander?"

"No, I discovered the secret passageways by accident. I was leaning against the wall in a chair one day when a rat scurried by. He disappeared and I went to investigate. It's amazing what gets your attention when you have nothing to entertain you." Howard swallowed the rest of his sandwich and reached into the fridge for a couple of sodas.

Marilyn held her hand out for one. He carefully put one in her palm without touching her then turned to the counter for a rag.

"I know many famous people have been here visiting Onassis. Have you seen or heard anything from them?"

"Yes, I've seen everyone from the Greek elite to the American version of royalty, including Jacqueline Kennedy." He wiped his hands for what seemed like a full minute before he turned to look at the wall clock.

"So what have you heard? Will you tell me?" Marilyn leaned closer to him, but he backed away, grabbing a Kleenex out of his pocket as he did.

"We better get back before they come to check on us. I'll show you the way so that you can come get your own meals from now on. You're dirty and I don't want to get sick."

"Thanks." Marilyn smiled at him; *he's certainly a whack job.*

Bobby shook hands with J. Edgar Hoover, "Well this is certainly something I never dreamed I would do." Bobby chuckled as the two men sat down at the diner.

"Well, it's time to iron a few things out. We're both practical men working for the good of our country. I disagree with you on most things, Kennedy, but for now I'm open to hear what you have to say." Hoover had opened the menu and began looking it over carefully.

Bobby ignored Hoover's comment and decided on what he wanted for his meal. After the waiter had taken orders and delivered drinks, Bobby turned his attention back to Hoover.

"I've heard that you have a hatred for the Greek bastard as deep as mine."

Hoover barked his laughter, "Blunt and to the point I see."

Bobby waited for an answer. Hoover sobered, steepled his fingers and leaned his chin on the indexes. "It's true."

"Then it appears we have a common enemy."

"In this one thing you are right, Kennedy."

"I'm right in another thing as well. We need to keep the failed Castro death plot a secret. It would harm our government a great deal for the Soviets to catch wind of it."

"Why is that? Castro is currently funding the overthrow of the premier. Surely the Soviets would appreciate it if Castro were to die after the dissidents take over otherwise they will still have a communist leader. I would want him dead, if I were the dissidents." Hoover wrinkled his brow in confusion.

"It would if they didn't have a double agent working in the premier's office. This person is someone we have always considered a friend and now we must tread carefully to avoid any scandal. Our friend in Russia is working with Castro to over throw his own government."

"Then we must insure this secret is well guarded, what do you propose we do about it?"

Papa Doc shouted at Onassis, "What do you mean you didn't send this telegram? I've been holding off going to see her because you told me too."

"God damn it, I did not. You're the idiot. Here's exactly what I sent you. I have the confirmation right here. I said," Onassis picked up the paper and read it word for word, "Got it on the island. Please be my guest. Servants alerted for your arrival. Enjoy."

"That is not what you sent me. You're an idiot." Papa Doc grabbed his telegram and read it, "Got it on the island. Stop. Wait for package to be unwrapped. Stop. Will alert you when it's clear. Stop."

"Bull shit." Onassis exploded, "Why would I send you that load of crap?"

"Do I need to make a voo doo doll of you, Onassis and torture you? Would you like to end up like your hated American president? You should know better than to lie to me."

"I would never lie to you, Duvalier." Onassis took a deep breath, "Son of a bitch, we've been found out!"

"Then I better get to that island of yours and find out who the damned whore is." Papa Doc slammed down the phone, "Pack my bags and ready my plane. I must leave at once!" He yelled at the poor fellow standing in the doorway.

Barbara Hadley knocked on the front door. As the butler opened the door she barreled her way into the house. "Where is my patient? Where is Ms. Baker?"

Chapter 37

April 22, 1964

Lyndon Johnson stood before the microphone at the opening ceremonies of the World's Fair, "And all of these dreams and these hopes and these expectations depend upon a world that is free from the threat of war. If we can achieve this..." as Lyndon droned on, he scanned the audience.

His gaze fell to an ugly familiar face as he finished his speech, "...and so I take my leave hoping and trusting that in the future it will not take anyone forty years to reach it. Thank you very much."

As Johnson stepped off the stage to applause, Lady Bird met him, smiled up at him and linked her arm in the crook of his elbow. "Very nice, Lyndon." She patted him as they walked toward the side of the stage.

Sam Giancana strode toward the couple. The secret service men had flanked the president and first lady as they stepped into the crowd.

"A word, Mr. President?" Sam watched as Johnson stepped away from his wife, she slowly released her hold on his arm with a worried look.

"Of course," Johnson nodded to the men and stepped a few paces away.

"You know things are taking much longer than we agreed to. My boss is not happy with the lack of progress. We have protected you from slander regarding the Bobby Baker scandal and the kickbacks from the Serve-U-Corp."

"Yes, you have," Johnson acknowledged with a nod, "But what do you want me to do at this point?"

"We took care of you, Johnson so that you could take care of us." Sam dropped his cigarette on the ground at Johnson's feet and stubbed it out with his booted toe. "Consider this warning number two, there will not be a third. Now as in this week my boss must see forward movement." Sam paused a moment and held Lyndon's gaze, "My boss needs his ships moving in the ocean, his drugs getting sold to help the wounded and our pockets lined with money in this 'Golden Triangle', his words not mine. I would hate to see anything happen to you as well, Mr. President."

Lady Bird had walked up to her husband during this speech. "Why, thank you. I worry about Lyndon all the time and it's refreshing to know I'm not the only one." She smiled and held out her hand to Sam who shook it with a startled expression. He then turned and melted into the crowd.

Jackie entered the garden through the terraced walkway. "Hi Bobby, you know how I hate these open parties."

Bobby hugged her and kissed her cheek, "Well, thanks for coming today. I know what it means to Lady Bird. It's a big occasion for the first ladies."

"Yes, but the Botanical Gardens attract so many bees." Jackie pulled her shades down her nose to look at Bobby. Just then Ethel rejoined her husband with Lady Bird in tow.

The women exchanged socially polite greetings as Jackie grabbed Bobby by the arm, "Show me where the refreshments are."

Ethel contained her anger as Bobby shrugged to her and walked away with Jackie.

"I know it was Jack who called. Why do you keep telling me it wasn't?" Jackie tugged on his sleeve.

"Because, it couldn't have been him. It was a prank, nothing more."

"But Bobby, I don't understand how he knew things about our honeymoon. It had to be Jack."

"Don't be ridiculous, Jackie, you yourself pulled his brain matter off the back of the limo. You know he's gone. Have you been to see anyone? Perhaps you need meds to help you through your trauma." Bobby patted her arm and smiled with sympathetic patience.

The private jet had taken off and the men sat back drinking brandy and smoking Cuban cigars. Jack put his feet up in the seat across from him as Bill stretched his out in the aisle and sighed.

"Thank God I'm finally out of that awful country." Bill took a deep cleansing breath.

"Okay, Bill, spill it. What's going on here? Why was it so urgent to get out of there?" Jack took a drag of his cigar and blew smoke toward the little window glancing out at the clear grey sky.

"This whole story actually begins with Nosenko. He brought word to the Embassy Khrushchev had no knowledge of Oswald's participation in your death. The two were completely unrelated as much as Castro tried to make it seem that they were."

"What the hell?"

"What that really means is Castro is the one who is behind Oswald's obsession and Castro used him to do his dirty work." Walton paused for Jack's reaction.

"Yes but it isn't anything we didn't already know." Jack picked up his brandy. "Surely there is more."

"Give me a minute to finish the points." Bill sipped his drink and leaned back, "What the United States didn't know is that this was a well-played plot to get you out of the picture, as well as to get Khrushchev overthrown and allow Castro to work his magic with the dissidents."

"Damn it, I know that too, tell me something I don't know, will you?" Jack fidgeted took a drink, and tapped his fingers on the little side window with impatience.

"Patience, Jack. Nosenko knew there was a spy in the Soviet government who was working for the United States and for Cuba."

"Of course there was, there are spies in every country; passing information all over the globe."

Bill ignored the interruption, "That spy has been feeding all secrets to those three countries for the money. Apparently he has been paid millions for his information. What our spy didn't realize is the U.S. Embassy had been bugged and his information was no longer needed."

"Now, I'm interested. What does it all mean?" Jack leaned forward.

"It means we now have definitive proof as to who wanted you dead." Bill paused to make sure he had Jack's attention, "And why they wanted to get Johnson in office. As well as what that would mean for the world and where we are headed as a nation."

"So who is behind it?"

"One guess," Bill took a sip his drink.

"Onassis?" Jack puffed his cigar steadily.

"Mostly, it was Georgi that tipped him off. Johnson could be bought with little effort because he hated being the vice president."

"True and he was always letting me know he didn't have anything legit to do as vice president so I made up stuff for him to do." Jack grimaced at the memory.

Bill nodded, "Johnson was already in trouble over various kickbacks so it was a matter of a little bribe from Onassis. He also had much to gain in the arming and munitions for the 'war'. His company will be one of the main ones used to arm the enemy."

"Shit!" Jack leaned forward nearly bumping heads with Bill in the cramped space.

"Most men would jump through hoops for that alone but Johnson wanted the presidency more than the money he stands to make from this deal. Johnson is in it for the power."

"And Onassis?" Jack sat back in his seat and took a drag on his cigarette.

"Onassis hopes to gain a shipping monopoly in the United States through his association with Johnson. He failed to realize the influence Bobby would have with Hoffa or that he would be balked in general by our government. No one trusts Onassis."

"That's true." Jack thought about it for a few moments, "Why kill me? He won't get any further with Johnson at the helm than he did with me. Doesn't Onassis realize there is only so much a president can do?"

"He's shrewd and knows that but he's counting on public opinion changing."

"And why would it change?"

"Because he's in pursuit of a certain beautiful grieving widow who is lost in Camelot."

Chapter 38

Howard Hughes watched from behind a secret passage through the small hole in the eyes of a portrait at the end of the hallway as the efficient looking woman strode toward Marilyn's room.

In the past few hours the Mormon mafia had moved Marilyn to the upstairs portion of the house and given her a beautiful room with a view of the ocean.

Howard had watched the proceedings with interest. As the door opened to Marilyn's new room, the nurse disappeared into the room and out of his view.

He slid the cover back over the 'eyes' of the portrait and slowly went back to his own dingy room. *I wonder if she came on a plane. I'd really like to fly again. Just a little spin couldn't hurt anything.*

Maybe I'll go check it out after they come to bring my lunch. Oh this could be so exciting. To fly, soar with the birds, feel that freedom just me and the sky. Yes! I must see. I'll take an entire box of Kleenex with me. Who knows what those germy bastards have brought here. Nasty people with nasty germs in a nasty world.

"Barbara!" Marilyn squealed as she recognized the woman who had just entered her room. She jumped up from the window seat, tossed the magazine aside and ran to hug her friend.

"Hi yourself!" Barbara laughed as the two exchanged a long hug.

"How did you get here?" Marilyn stepped back and gave her friend the once over.

"Bobby called me."

"Of course he would. I'm so glad to see you." Marilyn took Barbara by the hand and led her back to the window seat. "What's the plan?"

"First things first," Barbara sat down and crossed her legs, "You look okay. Are you being treated well?"

"I'm fine. You'll never guess who's here."

"Who?"

"Howard Hughes." Marilyn blurted.

"No! I thought he was in hiding in Hollywood."

"Well he's been here since the late fifties. Apparently his reclusive ways have kept people from questioning his whereabouts too closely."

"Oh my!" Barbara leaned back against the window frame, "How did he get here?"

"Same way as I did. The Mormon Mafia, of course." Marilyn grimaced as she flexed her hand still wrapped in a bandage.

"We can worry about him later." Barbara leaned closer to her, "Now here's the real problem. Papa Doc saw you on stage in Paris and he's convinced that you're Marilyn Monroe."

Marilyn laughed out loud at the statement, "How ridiculous."

Bobby lay cuddled next to Ethel. He breathed in the scent of her shampoo and sighed.

Ethel snuggled closer to him, "What's on your mind, Bob?"

"I have to go out of town for a few nights and I don't want to leave you." Bobby stroked her hair with practiced tenderness.

"I certainly don't want you to go. Is it somewhere I can go with you?"

"No. Not this time, honey. Who would watch the kids anyway? You'll have more fun at home with our brats."

"We could always ask Jackie to watch them." Ethel mocked.

"Don't be that way honey, you know how she is. She likes it peaceful and our brood is rowdy and unruly, just the way we love it." Bobby kissed the back of her neck.

"Still, her words stung, Bobby. She needn't have been so cruel about it. We were trying to be generous. Why didn't she simply say 'no, thank you'?" Ethel turned in his arms so he could kiss her properly.

"Do you really want to spend our last evening together for a few days discussing your sister-in-law?" he asked as he untied her nightgown.

"Is it?" Barbara stared intently at Marilyn, "Is it ridiculous?"

"Of course it is." Marilyn gave short nervous laugh.

"Uh huh and I'm a virgin." Barbara smiled, "I've known from the beginning who you are."

Marilyn blushed to the roots of her hair, "Really? Why didn't you tell me?"

"I thought you would tell me, but you never did." Barbara sounded hurt.

"I couldn't tell you even though I really wanted to." Marilyn hugged her friend, "No one is supposed to know I'm still alive."

Barbara nodded as Marilyn continued, "How could I tell you when I'd sworn to Bobby I would never tell a soul?"

"I understand." Barbara smiled at Marilyn, "I'm just glad that it's finally out. One of these days you'll have to tell me all about what has been going on with you for the past year."

"Deal," Marilyn held out her hand and the girls shook on it, "Now about Papa Doc."

"He wants to talk to you and if you're who he thinks you are he'll probably kill you."

"I was an actress I can fake it."

"No, it's too dangerous. We're leaving at dark."

"I think Johnson understands his position now." Giancana told Castro over cigars at a bar in Cuba.

"For your sake, my friend I certainly hope so." Castro downed his drink, wrinkled his forehead and stared at Sam for a moment.

"What?"

"I need you to find Marita."

Sam remained silent.

"She's in the United States, in New York City to be accurate, at least the last time my spies spotted her that is where she was." Castro held up his hand for another round of drinks, "She needs to return some valuable files she has stolen from me, that cunning little whore. Once those have been returned do with her whatever you see fit."

216

"When was the last sighting in New York and where?" Sam picked up a peanut and crushed it in his powerful palm.

"In a little café off of 5th. Nothing else. No address." Castro smirked, "I'll be eternally grateful for your assistance." He slid a small dirty envelope toward Sam.

Sam placed it in a jacket pocket, nodded and left the bar.

Chapter 39

Howard Hughes jumped onto the military jet, the L-29 Delfin he had had the pleasure of test flying in the later part of 1957 before they were pressed into service. He smiled; *I remember this wonderful little jet. The Czechoslovikian's were so nice to me and they're much less germy than other cultures. How wonderful I can take this little darling for a spin. I've wanted to fly one again.*

He settled himself into the cockpit and did his preflight check list. Once all the instruments were checked and he logged his information into the little book, Howard pressed the ignition button.

The piston engine roared to life as he clapped his hands, "Yes!" The feel of the powerful engine vibrated through the cockpit.

He pushed the throttle forward and the plane taxied down the short runway but he didn't gain speed. "No matter, this little baby will take off from any surface."

As he made his way down the airstrip he taxied off the runway and down to a strip of beach just past the house. "I've always wanted to test a beach take off. Let's do it." He patted the little plane's console as he began to bump over the grassy yard in front of Marilyn's windows.

Kenny watched as Lady Bird marched into his office, plopped herself down in the chair and sighed. "Well, that was a completely wasted trip." She began as he closed the file folder on his desk and gave her his full attention.

"Why would a trip to the World's Fair be wasted?" Kenny leaned on his elbow and tapped the end of his pen against the notepad on his desk.

"Because there were few actual carnival rides and it was all about commerce and industry. Lyndon wouldn't even stay for a few minutes after his speech so I could ride the Ferris Wheel. I love the Ferris Wheel. That man is just so self-centered sometimes. Would it have killed him to indulge me a little?" Lady Bird had sat her little purse on her lap and began pulling off her crisp white gloves.

"I'm sure he had his reasons." Kenny shrugged.

"Yes, that nasty Mr. Giancana ruined everything."

"Sam Giancana?"

"Yes. Right after Lyndon's speech he approached us. Once they had talked we had to leave right away. Lyndon would hear none of my protests and was truly quite rude to me. He even grabbed my elbow and pulled me along to the limo." Lady Bird folded the gloves neatly into her purse and looked pointedly at the coffee pot on the table beside Kenny.

"Would you care for some coffee or tea, Mrs. Johnson?' he asked, *When did I become her confidant?*

"Yes, that would be lovely. You know how I like it." Lady Bird crossed her ankles and watched him prepare her cup. "Why does everyone say that Lyndon has mafia ties?"

Kenny nearly spilled the coffee into the saucer at her abrupt question. He placed the coffee pot back in its holder and handed her the cup and saucer. "Who says that?"

"Thank you," Lady Bird took the offered drink. "I've heard he's been linked to the mafia and they've been the driving in force in his dropped charges for kickbacks and political favors. He's an honest man, my Lyndon, though I don't understand all of these political things. It was much easier when he was just a powerful Texan."

"Why do you think charges were brought against him?" Kenny sat back down at his desk, leaned his elbows on it and watched her sip her coffee.

"Jealousy, plain and simple, there is no other reason."

"So that is why the charges were dismissed? They were unfounded?"

"Yes, of course, my Lyndon would never do anything dishonest. He's not like that."

"I understand your loyalty to your husband and it's an admirable trait in a wife. I'm sure he is proud of you." Kenny smiled.

"Thank you, young man. You're pleasant to talk to. I always feel better once we've had our little chats." Lady Bird placed her coffee cup on the side table at her elbow and pulled her gloves out of her purse.

"Mrs. Johnson, could you tell me what Mr. Giancana told your husband at the World's Fair?"

"He just said he needed Lyndon to return some favor he had done for him. He said Lyndon knew what he needed and when." Lady Bird had put her gloves back on and stood up. "Thank you. Now I must be off to find material for a new dress."

Kenny stood up as she prepared to leave, "Have a great afternoon, Mrs. Johnson."

As she was about to exit through his door, she stopped and turned back to him. "He did say he would hate to see anything happen to my Lyndon like what happened to poor Mr. Kennedy."

Barbara was staring out at the beautiful ocean as the plane went taxing by the window. "What the hell!"

Marilyn jumped up from the bed and raced to the window, she pulled back the curtain staring as the little plane bumped down the beach for a few moments and then ascended over the water.

"Who in the hell took my plane?" Barbara shrieked as she started toward the door.

Marilyn turned to Barbara with a stunned look, "Your plane?"

Barbara stopped and came back to Marilyn as she watched her plane soar over the sea, "Yes, that's my plane. I saved for years to buy it and now someone is stealing it. There's not even anyone to contact about it. You don't exist and I can't explain why I'm here." Barbara punched the glass of the window so hard it broke.

"It looked like Howard." Marilyn tried to reassure her, "I bet he just wanted to fly it."

"But it's not his to 'borrow'. It's my prized possession. How dare he?" Barbara leapt into action and headed to the door. "I'm going to strangle him with my bare hands if he ever comes back with my plane." Furious, she took off at a run down the hall and out into the yard.

Two Mormon mafia men chased after her, "What's going on?"

"That lunatic stole my plane!" Barbara pointed in the direction of the now barely visible tail of her plane. "Do something, you morons!"

"What can we do?"

"Go after him you buffoon!"

"Can't, I don't have anything to chase him with. Who took it anyway?" The man with a bandaged nose placed his hand over his eyes to shield them from the glare of the sun.

Barbara stared at him, "How many people are on this island that can fly a plane?"

"Well, you and Hughes." He answered looking up at the sky.

"Okay, genius, I'm standing here so who do you think took MY plane?"

Jack Lancer stepped off the plane behind Bill Walton after they had landed on a tiny little airstrip on a tropical islet near the islands of Hawaii.

No one had met them as they left the tarmac and walked up to the hut that doubled as the airport. Jack looked around at the seemingly tropical paradise and followed Bill up the short sandy path.

Bill walked into the little building and grabbed a key ring off the table. Not a single person could be seen anywhere. Jack looked around the dingy little room with a few small windows open to the breeze.

"Where are we?"

"We have arrived at Palmyra Atoll. It's owned by our government but not lived on by any permanent residents. There is a small home over on the other side of the islet. Currently we are the only ones here." Bill explained as they walked to a couple of bicycles parked near the door of the hut.

"I hope you haven't forgotten how to ride." Bill popped the kickstand, jumped on the bike and rode toward the sandy bricks which served as a walkway for the little strip of land.

"I hope not either." Jack muttered as he pushed his bike out the door and hopped onto the torn seat.

Tropical flowers grew wild as the ocean rushed up to the shores. The air was so muggy it felt like it would rain any second. The islet was silent except for the sounds of nature. The humidity made their shirts stick to their backs.

Jack rode along behind Bill for a few moments taking it all in before he interrupted the solitude.

"Why are we here?" Jack finally turned to Bill.

"We're meeting Norma and Bobby if things went well. They should be here in a couple of days. Until then we relax and enjoy doing nothing."

"If no one is here what do we do for food?"

"We fish and eat the fruit. I hope you like pineapples and mangos."

"Sure."

"We can swim and just do nothing. I'm tired." Bill pedaled a little slower as his energy was sapped in the muggy heat of the afternoon.

"Great! Just what I wanted, a deserted island," Jack scoffed. "Where is the pretty Hawaiian woman in the grass skirt? Now that is my kind of deserted island."

Bill laughed, "Sorry pal, no women."

"What the hell is happening to me? I have no say or control over anything. I'm used to calling the shots. This is bullshit."

"Look, Jack, I know this must be hard for you but just try and relax until Bobby gets here. Okay?"

"I can't just sit back and let someone else run the show. I'm not built that way. Why *wasn't* it me shot in that limo?"

Chapter 40

Clark Gifford stepped up beside Lyndon Johnson in the park on the Potomac River.

"Lyndon."

"Clark, I'm glad you could meet me here today." Johnson continued to stare out at the river.

"It must be important if you wanted to meet this far from the White House." Clark took out his cigarette case and extracted one, then tapped it on the edge of the railing.

"You understand me all too well, Clark. That's why I always call on you when things are getting muddled." Johnson watched a group of ducks swim past.

"Get to the point, Lyndon. I don't have all day to play games even if you are the president." Clark put the case away and withdrew his lighter from the inside pocket of his jacket, "You've been my friend far longer than you've had this job and I know you didn't call me here for idle chit chat." Clark laughed and lit the cigarette.

Johnson turned to face Clark, "Here's the deal that's going down. Haiti is the biggest problem on my agenda right now. Duvalier has financial needs that I don't know how to meet. He's offering to help me with the communism issue that Castro continues to provide. Now that the dissidents are stirring up in Russia it looks like Khrushchev will be overthrown." Johnson took a deep breath and plunged on, "However, Duvalier says all my problems will disappear if we fund his little island of Haiti." Johnson got out his own packet of cigarettes and opened the fresh pack.

"You do have a problem. How did you get into this mess?" Clark blew out smoke and watched the gulls land on the shore near the water.

"John Kennedy was shot and that is how I landed in this trouble. What do you think?" Lyndon snipped as he put the cigarette to his lips and lit it.

"Damn, you really don't handle pressure well do you?" Clark shook his head, "What happens when you can't bully someone to do your bidding?"

"What happens, Clark is I call you. Now how are you going to help me handle this? I need funds to somehow be funneled to Haiti. I don't want to know how they get there or where those funds come from. I just need you to handle it. Can you do that?"

"I can do that but it'll cost you." Clark smiled as he dropped his cigarette on the ground and put it out with his shoe.

Clint Hill stood at the front door waiting on someone to answer the secret knock he had been given. As he looked around the large front yard he noticed nothing remarkable about the house or its surroundings.

It looked like any other farm he'd been to except this one is where they trained the agents for the CIA, a non-assuming house in everyday America would hardly bring attention.

The door opened and Clint showed his badge. He was let in without a word and led down a short hallway, down the stairs and into a finished basement area.

The guard opened the door and motioned Clint into the room. He closed the door behind Hill so quickly that he barely had time to get his coat tail away from the door frame.

Nosenko sat on a well-worn couch watching a black and white television set with rabbit ears covered in aluminum foil sitting on top of it. 'The Price is Right' was on the set with host Bill Cullen announcing the next contestant.

Hill moved into the room and sat beside Nosenko on the couch. As he settled himself, Nosenko glanced at him.

"Hello, I'm Clint Hill. It's nice to meet you Mr. Nosenko." He held out his hand for Yuri to shake.

Yuri sat up a bit straighter and placed his hand in Hill's. "Hello, Mr. Hill. What has brought you all the way out here on this lovely day?" the sarcasm oozed through Nosenko's voice.

"It has come to our attention that you may be able to help us out with a guest in our country. Perhaps you wouldn't mind giving me some information about her."

"I'll be happy to help you, Mr. Hill as long as I'm guaranteed no misuse. Forgive me if I don't exactly trust your government or this country to protect my person from being beaten."

"I do understand and I actually appreciate your concerns. While it is beyond my ability to help you in that regard I can offer to put in a good word for you if you do help me out." Clint smiled a little to reassure him.

"How can I help you with your problem?" Yuri asked. "Clearly I'm no longer providing information to anyone."

"Fidel Castro's girlfriend has gone missing. Rumor has it she is in the United States. I know you had met with her in Russia before you came here."

Yuri watched Hill but didn't blink or comment on these accusations.

"Do you know where she is now? She's in danger from the Cuban mafia. Castro has sent his henchmen over here to get her."

"Marita?"

"Yes."

Yuri's eyes widened, "Shit."

"Can you help me?"

"I know where she is, yes, but how do I know you will not protect her in the same manner I'm being protected?" Yuri shook his head in bewilderment, "Everyday I'm questioned, the same questions that I've been asked a thousand times over and then if my answers do not meet with the approval of the inquisitor another takes his place. At least Joannides was true to his words and the beatings have stopped, but I'm never really sure if they will resume."

Clint flinched a little at this speech, but refused to be diverted, "I'm personally going to go and get Marita. Her situation is different from yours. She is being hunted for Castro's gain. She did not defect from her country. She's a guest here in this country and we will protect her if we can find her."

Chapter 41

Papa Doc stood on the deck of his yacht waiting to dock on the little Greek island where he knew the woman known as Norma Baker was being held. "What the hell is going on? Let's get this mother docked."

One of the crew men came running up to him, "I'll find out right away." He took off running and left Papa Doc standing on the deck shielding his eyes.

An erratically flying plane buzzing the shoreline seemed the most obvious reason for the delay. The plane made a bouncing bumpy landing near the airstrip but not on it.

As soon as it landed, the pilot jumped out of the plane and took off running. Papa Doc noticed a couple of men in suits chase after him. He watched for a few moments until they all disappeared around the corner of the house.

Howard laughed wildly as the two men chased him. "You can't catch me! You can't touch me! You don't have any gloves on." He raced wildly around the sand until he had them tripping over their own feet. He sprinted towards the house leaving them trying to regain their footing.

He stopped on the opposite side of the house and slid into the basement through a secret opening in the vines growing up the side of the house.

"Where did the bastard go?" They looked at each other and then around at the vines and shrubs, beating at the bushes they crawled on suited knees looking for any signs of foot prints.

"Shit, we're in for it now."

They could be heard yelling at each other just out of Howard's view. *That was truly wonderful. It's been far too long since I've had the controls of a jet in my hands.*

He walked down the darkened narrow passageway back to the wooden wall that opened a few feet from his own room. Silently he opened the door and checked the hallway, it was clear.

He slid out of the secret passage into the hall, crossed into his room and sunk onto his bed. *They never saw me up close and can't really know if it was me or not. Stupid idiots, you may be strong but I'm smarter.* He reached for a clean shirt, changed quickly and put the other one in a laundry hamper nearby. He kicked off his shoes and lay down just a second before the door opened.

Marita hunkered down behind the first dumpster in the alley as the four men walked quickly past on the sidewalk. They had been following her for a few blocks when she noticed them in the store window. *I knew it. It is way too hot for them to be out for a casual stroll in those heavy suits and ugly ties. They're looking for me.*

She watched as two of the men walked back past the alley and then suddenly came rushing past her hiding place, scaring a few stray rats into scurrying away.

They walked up and down the alley looking in corners and nooks but they didn't check behind the dumpsters pushed close against the brick walls.

As they left the alley, Marita let out the breath she'd been holding and allowed a single tear to roll down her cheek. *I've got to find a safe place to hide. Holy mother please help me.*

Barbara noticed the boat waiting to moor and grabbed Marilyn by the arm, "We have to go. Now!" She pointed towards the dock as the women took off running, "Duvalier."

Marilyn ran beside Barbara as they approached the small jet plane that had just landed. "Let's hope that bastard left us enough fuel to get to safety."

A worried Marilyn jumped into the co-pilot seat. She ducked down under the console as Barbara started up the plane and they taxied onto the short runway. As they began to ascend Barbara noticed the yacht had docked and a portly man was disembarking onto the wooden planks that led to the shore.

"But darling, why can't you break away for a long weekend with me?" Ari sat at the hotel in France, holding the receiver of the telephone.

"Because I promised Caroline I would take her to the country where she can get away from the ridicule of her classmates. It's turned into a nightmare for her. Her father's death is still painful for her and the kids at school have begun taunting her about it." Jackie tried to explain as she picked lint off of her perfect pink sweater.

"You could bring the children with you to France and they could shop. I would hire a nanny to watch them while we make up for lost time."

"Ari, I hate to disappoint you but I have other commitments right now."

"I'm an impatient man at times, my dear." Ari sighed masking the threat.

"It would be lovely," she conceded, "but I just can't right now. I'm trying to be the good mother everyone expects me to be. They need me." Jackie sighed, "Though I'd much rather be eating crepes and drinking champagne with you."

"What do you know about Howard Hunt?" Nosenko asked as Hill returned with a full cup of coffee for both of them.

"I know he's in the Central Intelligence Agency as an agent. He's been involved with some money laundering as well as rumored to be involved with Fidel Castro although nothing has been proven." Hill answered honestly.

"If I give you some information I know you will find most useful, will you make sure I won't be tortured any longer? I've proven I truly want to be a citizen of this country and have endured the agony dished out to me every day. What more do they want from me?" Nosenko sipped his coffee while Hill thought about his offer.

"I will see what I can do. I'll make a strong case for you and try to pull a few strings to have you left alone." Hill held out his hand. Yuri slowly reached out and took it.

"Howard Hunt is a double agent for Castro. His code name is Eduardo. Marita saw Hunt give money to Jack Ruby in Dallas. That is why she is running. She didn't know he was so deeply involved with the Cuban mafia."

"Go on."

"Have you ever stopped to wonder why your government hasn't been successful in killing Castro despite your numerous attempts?"

"Of course we have, our plans are generally carried out without a hitch."

"Did you not wonder why the Bay of Pigs was such a fiasco?" Nosenko placed his coffee cup on the table in front of him.

"Yes, we did but we've never been able to find out why Castro was elsewhere when our intel had been insistent he was there."

"Why don't you ask your good friend Howard Hunt?" Nosenko returned to watching television as the contestants finished the showcases on 'The Price is Right'.

"Thanks, Mr. Nosenko. I'll see what I can do for you and Marita." Hill stood up to take his leave, "Where is she? Do you have an address for her?"

"She's in New York, in the Hoboken area. You'll be able to find her at this address, 4112 Elm."

"Thank you."

"Be sure and tell Marita I've repaid her debt and I no longer owe her a favor. Just keep her safe."

"You have my word."

Chapter 42

Frank Sinatra had just finished with a scene for the movie, 'None but the Brave'.

"I love Hawaii!" Frank sighed as a couple of bikini clad beauties hung on his arm. "Anyone up for a swim?"

"Sure Frank, can you spare one of your dames?" Clint Walker came toward them stripping off his World War II costume and revealing his gorgeous upper body to the women following Frank.

Frank laughed and said, "Of course Big Guy, I'll even let you pick as long as you leave these two alone."

"Funny. I would never dream of taking either of these dolls. There's enough trailing on your heels to pick from." Clint flexed his muscles and three women came running up to him. "Problem solved."

Frank and Clint walked to the beach with several beautiful groupies following along.

"Hey, what is that little strip of land over there? I just saw a plane land." Clint shielded his eyes to get a better view.

"That's an Atoll. I think it's called Palmyra or something. The islanders talk about it being deserted. We could take a boat over there in a few days when we wrap this thing." Frank leaned down to kiss one of the girls on the cheek. She turned his head and he kissed her full on the mouth.

"Maybe." Clint laughed at his distracted director.

Lyndon Johnson sat in the limo waiting for Walter Jenkins to get in the car. Johnson had ordered a stretch limo with privacy glass to drive them around the D.C. area for this secret meeting.

Walter got into the car as the driver closed the door for him. He slid across the seat and faced the president. As the car eased into traffic, Lyndon leaned back, crossed his arms, and gave Jenkins the once over.

"Walter I've asked you for this meeting because I need someone I can trust. I believe you're my man."

"I'll do anything for my country, Mr. President. You know I would also do anything for you, no matter what you asked within my power."

"Good. Now what I need from you is a strategy for a military battle. Can you handle that?"

"I need more details, but I think it's something I can work out." Jenkins leaned closer to the president.

"This is top secret information and you will be the only other person who knows about this intel. Should it leak to the public in any way I'll know it was from you. Are we clear?"

"Yes, Mr. President. What can I help you with?" Walter loosened his tie and moved over to make himself a drink from the small sidebar in the limo.

"I need to move some key people into position in our military branches. I've already chosen the man who will handle the satellite images we need, the radar technician. But now I need a good general in my corner. How can we 'promote' General Paul Harkins to the Head of U. S. Forces in Vietnam?"

Walter sat for a moment sipping his drink. "I'll just make a recommendation and it will be finalized. He's nearly there as it is and everyone turns to him. He's a hater of communism which makes him an extremely likeable guy in our military."

"Yes, we all hate communism, Mr. Jenkins, this knowledge you have is exactly why I have called upon you for help. I knew you had a good head on your shoulders and a mind for military matters." Lyndon smiled at him and relaxed a little. "I have been receiving pressure from our foreign friends to do something about Vietnam. They are tired of this little 'non-war'."

"Understood, Mr. President. What else would you have me help you with?"

"I need to figure out how to get our troops into the fray and escalate this into a full scale war. The pressure to end this conflict is immense and as you know our former commander and chief wanted nothing to do with war."

"Have you considered General Maxwell Taylor; he'd best serve you as the Ambassador for the US Envoy. He'd been bucking to put troops in even while Kennedy was saying no."

"I believe he would be a great asset to our mission."

Marilyn searched through the luggage Barbara had brought for her. She found a large pair of sunglasses, her make up case and a head scarf. She pulled out the vanity case and looked in the mirror. "Lord, Barbara, you don't need to worry about anyone recognizing me. I don't even recognize myself. I look awful."

Barbara glanced over at Marilyn, momentarily taking her eyes from the controls of the jet. "We need fuel soon. Be a good co-pilot and pull out that map."

Marilyn wiped at her face with a Kleenex as she turned in her seat to get the map, she grabbed it and unfolded it. "What am I looking for?"

"Somewhere close with an airstrip and private not public. We don't want any of Onassis' goons catching sight of us."

"How do I know where an airstrip is?" Marilyn turned the map, found the general area they were in and folded it smaller to get a closer look at a where they were heading.

"There's a little marking on it, over on the side with a key to the map. You better hurry we're really low on fuel. Damn that joyriding Hughes!"

Bobby's plane landed on Palmyra. Jack and Bill Walton had seen the plane coming and rode their bikes over to the airstrip to greet the plane.

Jack looked like an islander with his cut-off pants and shirtless physique.

As Bobby stepped out of the plane, the pilot began unloading crates. The boxes were piled on the ground near the plane followed by a golf cart that had been modified to resemble the back of a small pick-up truck.

When Jack spotted his brother placing boxes on the golf cart he jumped off the bike and ran the last few yards to Bobby, "Bobby! Oh thank God."

Bobby turned around just in time to be swept into the embrace of his older brother. "Jack!"

The two men stood hugging each other for a long moment before leaning back, still holding onto each other. "It's great to see you, Bobby." Jack finally released his brother and stepped back.

"You're looking robust. I'm glad to see the surgery did what it was supposed to."

Jack hugged Bobby again. "I just can't believe you're here. I never thought I'd see you again."

"It's crazy to see you. Even though I knew you were alive. I almost believe you're dead myself some days. Everyone is still talking about it."

"I saw Jackie in Paris. What a nightmare." Jack sighed and impulsively hugged Bobby again. "Did you bring some meat? I'm sick of trying to catch fish and eating fruit. I need some protein!"

"Of course I did. There's milk, eggs, steak, potatoes and fresh cookies from Ethel's stock pile. She'll be annoyed when she's sees I've taken the entire batch."

Bill Walton had stood by while they had their reunion. "Hi, Bobby. Glad you decided to show up."

"You just wanted to eat something besides pineapples and coconuts." Bobby laughed as he shook Bill's hand.

"Damn right. I don't usually eat fruit. What did you bring?" Bill had begun looking at the boxes for a sign as to what all was in them. Jack and Bobby had been placing boxes on the golf cart as Bill poked around them.

"Patience, my friend," Bobby loaded the last box onto the golf cart and turned back to the pilot. "I'll be ready to go in the morning. Feel free to go visit Hawaii but don't go too far. Let's be fueled and ready to leave by 10. Okay?"

The pilot smiled, "You bet. I hear they are shooting a film over there and I want to see how it's done. See you tomorrow!"

Castro paced the large room. His cigar had burned down in his hand but he hadn't noticed. Johnson hadn't returned his call from last night. The phone rang and Fidel jumped to answer it.

"Hello."

"It's Sam. There is movement in the military. I think our friend is beginning to get this thing rolling. I'll keep you informed."

Chapter 43

"Barcelona has a small strip. Can we make it there?" Marilyn held on as the plane dipped a bit and shuddered.

"I hope so; we're almost out of fuel. I'll have to get up higher so we can glide to land."

Marilyn strapped herself into the parachute as Barbara pulled the throttle to gain altitude. "How many kilometers do we have? Notice the readings?" Barbara pointed to the gages.

"It looks like fifty."

"Good, now where is that airstrip located?"

"Jenkins, you managed to accomplish your task. How you did it so quickly is beyond me. Thank you." Johnson held out his hand to Walter.

"You're welcome, Mr. President. Is there anything else you need from me?"

"Yes. But first; congratulations on getting Henry Cabot Lodge to resign so peacefully, well done."

"Thank you." Walter looked at the ground at the unusual praise.

"Yes; and Taylor just moved naturally into his place. Excellent maneuvering. You obviously have a knack for military strategy." Johnson beamed at Walter.

Walter ran his finger around his collar, "You're welcome, again, Mr. President." He swallowed hard, "What can I do for you now?"

"General Westmoreland needs to be moved into position as Harkins' replacement. Focus on that now."

Walter relaxed as the praise was now turned to practical discussion, "You mean the Head of U. S. forces in Vietnam?"

"Yes. Surely you're not questioning my strategy? As a former war hero myself, I'm well aware of the best man for this job. Harkins must go and the general must take his place. Understood?"

"Definitely."

Frank had been swimming with his lady friends but now he lay on the beach soaking up the sun's rays. His producer, Howard Koch and his wife Ruth were still in the surf.

"Help!" Ruth called as she was caught in the current sucking her further out into the sea.

Frank jumped up and ran into the water. Ruth was struggling and Howard was trying to get to her. "I'm not strong enough." Howard panted as he tried to reach his wife.

Howard was treading water as Frank swam past him. Frank reached for Ruth's hand, her head was submerged. He managed to grab her fingers. She clasped his hand as he began pulling her to safety but the current sucked him under as well.

Papa Doc knocked on the door, when it opened he barked, "Onassis said I am expected. I want my room now and I'm in need of refreshment. My crew will bring my luggage shortly."

As Duvalier was ordering around the startled maid, the two Mormon mafia men ran past them and down a hallway, guns at the ready.

"What the hell is going on here?"

"I really don't know, your excellency but I think the woman is gone."

"Norma Baker?" Duvalier sputtered.

Holding onto Ruth, Frank fought and kicked hard to regain his way up to the top of the surf, while his lungs were ready to burst. He made it to the surface, took a breath just as he was sucked under again. Ruth had managed to get a shallow breath as well but she had stopped fighting him and lay limp in his grasp.

Suddenly, Frank lurched upward with his last bit of strength and got to the surface where Clint was within arm's length.

Clint pushed a surfboard toward Frank who grabbed onto it with his free hand. As Clint pulled Ruth onto the board and managed to get them all back to the shore Frank heaved a huge sigh of relief.

Jackie sat finishing her expensive dessert with Charlie Spalding as the waiter came by with the check. Lunch had been fantastic in an upscale D.C. restaurant and she had enjoyed it immensely.

"Thank you for inviting me to lunch today." Charlie smiled as he finished his coffee.

"It's always so nice to catch up with my friends." Jackie fished out her compact and a tube of lipstick.

"That's true. Now I really must return to the office. I must thank you again for the invitation. Kiss the kids for me." Charlie got up and left her with the check, grinning at his own cleverness, *I've turned the tables for once, eh Jackie.*

Shocked, Jackie just sat there as the waiter handed her the little silver plate for payment, *But I never pay.*

Barbara lowered the plane and bounced onto the runway. The plane was coming in too high and slow to make the landing easy. She managed to land the plane on the tiny airstrip just as the engine died and they rolled to a stop just off the other side of the tarmac.

Marilyn sobbed with relief as Barbara turned off the remaining gages and prepared to disembark.

"Great job." Marilyn managed through her tears.

"Thanks, I've been through worse landings. Now let's see who can help us get this bird refueled and on our way."

"Onassis! Get back to this god forsaken island right now!" Duvalier screamed into the phone receiver. He slammed it down and stormed into his room cursing in voo doo slang.

Marita left the beauty shop in Hoboken looking like a different woman. Her hair was cut and dyed dark blonde, her brows had been bleached and she received long false eyelashes the shade of her hair. For all intents she looked like an average American girl. She headed for the nearest coffee shop while scanning the crowds around her.

Melting into a booth, Marita ordered a sandwich and iced tea. A few seconds later she was startled as a man slid into the seat beside her. She tried to slide under the table but he grabbed her arm roughly and jerked her back into her seat.

"Smile," he demanded of her, "you should just act natural." His head shot toward the windows outside and the two men lurking around the window watching them.

Marita smiled and tried to look relaxed, "I'm smiling but you need to explain."

"I'm agent Clint Hill. Nosenko sent me to help you. Just keep smiling and everything will be all right. Laugh, like I just said something funny and put your hand on my arm."

She did and he released the arm he'd been holding to keep her from sliding under the table and leaving him.

"Nosenko?"

"Yes, as you know he owed you one. He says to tell you that you're even."

Marita smiled without being told and relaxed.

The waitress brought her order and got Hill a coffee and a piece of pie.

"Do you think they recognize me?" Marita asked as she lifted the sandwich for a bite.

"I don't think so. The only reason I did was because I followed you from the apartment you'd been living in."

"Where do we go from here?" Marita sipped her tea while Hill poured sugar into his coffee mug.
"To safety," Hill kissed her on the cheek, an unexpected move as the two goons on the sidewalk shrugged and walked away.

Chapter 44

Kenny O'Donnell finished tidying up his desk and switched off the small light over his typewriter. He rubbed his eyes and loosened his tie just as McGeorge Bundy came into the office.

"How's it going?" Bundy asked as Kenny picked up his briefcase and headed toward the door.

"Long story, want to join me for a drink?" Kenny allowed Bundy to leave the room first as Kenny placed the key in the lock and twisted it. He wiggled the door knob and pocketed the key.

"Sure, why not."

They walked down the hall together for a moment before Bundy spoke, "You know the Commission report was a lie, don't you?"

Kenny stopped walking and turned to Bundy, "What proof do you have? I've been looking into it for Bobby."

"I know there were two bullet holes in Kennedy. I also know that it was a mob hit." Bundy continued to walk down the hall forcing Kenny to keep up with his long strides.

"How do you know that?"

"Simple. Don't you think the incident with Frank Sinatra Jr. was a bit of a warning? Frank is acquainted with many in the mob and his ties run deep. Perhaps he knew something he shouldn't and that is why his son was kidnapped."

Kenny paused for a moment just on the outer steps as they left the building, "That could be."

"Why else would the media have gotten their teeth into the story and then turned it into a 'prank for publicity'?"

"I hadn't thought of that, but it makes sense."

"Kenny, you've a lot to learn. The media is run by the mob and its father the mafia. Don't you think for one moment that anything that hits the news is accidental. They control everything."

"But how would that tie into Frank Sinatra and his son?"

"Apparently, Frank had said something to someone that he shouldn't have and this was a warning that his family would be in danger if he didn't shut up. The question is; what does he know and who did he tell? My guess is that the answers to those two questions will bring the identity of the killer to light. Just because Oswald shot one of the bullets doesn't mean he was acting alone. What did he have to prove?"

"I guess we'll never really know, will we?" Kenny sidestepped a woman and her screaming child.

The men reached their favorite bar, and sat in a secluded booth in the back corner away from the crowd.

After ordering beer, Kenny broke the silence, "What you are suggesting is a full blown conspiracy, right?"

"Of course. There are only a few people in this world more powerful than the U. S. President and none of them are smarter than our intelligence agencies working on their own. This was a plot from the beginning and I think I know who the ring leader is."

Marilyn and Barbara entered the small airport in Barcelona hoping to find a bite to eat. While Barbara had taken care of the post flight logs, Marilyn had busied herself with a hairbrush and make-up, after she had changed into a clean pair of slacks and shirt. She added some lip gloss and smiled at her reflection in the tiny mirror.

As they made their way to the ladies room, a large group of rowdy football players walked past them, whistling and ogling as they headed for the bar area.

Marilyn just smiled and waved as Barbara turned beat red with embarrassment. "Wow, you've still got it." Barbara ducked into the restroom with her happy friend on her heels.

"Thank goodness. Give me ten minutes and they'll wonder what hit them." Marilyn giggled.

Hoover flipped through the pages of the newest findings in the Warren Commission late in the evening though he was not really reading them. *That son of a bitch, Johnson has Warren terrified. Where is the evidence of the other bullet? What about the mention of two different calibers?*

Hoover pulled on his nose with his index finger and thumb, in frustration. A shadow crossed his desk and he looked up, startled to find Jim Angleton.

"Hey. I've been following Mary Meyer but if you want what I've found out you'll have to pay up." Jim smiled seductively and leaned over the desk.

"I'm starving. Let's see what the bar has to offer." Marilyn led the way towards the rowdy football players.

"Yes, but what are you hungry for?" Barbara teased as Marilyn fluffed her hair.

"A little male flirtation and a free steak dinner of course, come on I'll show you how it's done."

Barbara smiled and walked behind her friend as they entered the bar. All of the men in the room turned to stare at the beautiful blonde who had just swayed her way into their hearts.

"Ari, I'm sorry to tell you this but I need more money. It just takes so much to run a household these days." Jackie pouted as she lay cuddled in his embrace.

"Of course darling, I'd give you the moon if I could." Ari stroked her bare back and kissed her lightly on the neck.

Jackie smiled into the darkness and prepared to thank him properly.

As the men surrounded them, Marilyn smiled and flirted while Barbara hung back a bit stunned.

"Hello there! I'm Fernando Martinez. Please, ladies, let us buy you a drink in honor of Spain winning the first ever football game against Soviet Union." Fernando smiled as he ushered the ladies to the bar.

"Well, honey," Marilyn smiled and batted her eyelashes, "I always hang out with the winners."

He pulled out the bar stool and seated her and then Barbara as the rest of the team gathered closely around them.

Laughter and flirting came so naturally to Marilyn that she didn't see how uncomfortable Barbara was for a few minutes.

"Barbara, would you like to go sit in a booth?" Marilyn leaned over to her friend and whispered loudly into her ear.

"No, you have fun. I'll just sit here and watch."

"You will not, I'll fix this in a jiffy." Marilyn scanned the men and her gaze landed on a familiar face in the crowd. She continued to smile but it now seemed fixed and false. Leaning back to Barbara, "I'm certain that is someone I know and don't want him to see me. I'm going to have to create a drastic situation."

"Do what you must."

Marilyn turned a blinding smile on the group of men standing around them. She wiggled off the bar stool and held up a finger for silence. They all leaned forward, to hear her softly spoken words, "Hey boys, who wants to buy us a steak dinner and win our company for a while?"

The men went nuts and Marilyn chose the two linebackers. They moved to a booth directly behind Sam Giancana and his friend. Marilyn sat with her back to Sam and the linebacker beside her while Barbara and her date sat on the opposite side of the table.

During dinner Sam got up and smiled at the Soviet, allowing Marilyn to overhear his words, "Leonid, I'll return in a moment but you know Castro is supporting you with Onassis' money to remove Khrushchev. Now average Soviets can live better and never worry again about living under a dictator like Stalin."

"I'll believe that when it happens. We have been lied to before. What makes this different?"

"Both Onassis and Castro hate the United States," Sam slipped back into the booth.

Marilyn leaned against her seat to hear the rest of the conversation, sighing that he hadn't seen her behind the big linebacker. *Can't I go anywhere on this planet without running into trouble?*

Onassis had just stepped off the private jet that brought him back to the island as Papa Doc stood glowering at him. "I've assembled the necessary ingredients for a voo doo curse. Quickly now we must hurry and perform the ceremony. Get those goons to help us."

"Hold up there, Duvalier, I may be willing to help you build Haiti into another Monaco but I'm not willing to help you put a curse on people who may or may not be who you think they are." Onassis stopped in front of Papa Doc, holding his ground.

"You have no power here Onassis, I'm the voodoo priest and unless you want to be cursed you'll do as I say." Papa Doc turned on his heel and marched down the tarmac toward the beach where a huge bonfire was ready to be lit.

Onassis caught up to him, "Duvalier, if you want Haiti to be anything but a poverty stricken pock on the world you'll listen to me. I'm not the one who needs to be afraid of a curse, my friend. No, sir, you should be terrified that I'll back away from your paltry little nation and leave it in squalor."

Chapter 45

Ethel held Christopher as Pat splashed in the pool with the other children. After a few minutes, Pat got out and sat in the chair beside Ethel, drying herself with a large warmed towel.

"I don't know how those kids don't freeze to death. It's too early to be in the pool." Pat grabbed the baby's discarded blanket and wrapped it around her legs.

"They're kids, what do they know?" Ethel laughed as she handed the baby off to the temporary nanny.

"I don't remember being that tough skinned." Pat picked up the coffee mug and took a warming sip.

"I've been thinking about Jackie and how calculating she is. Did you know she told Bobby after Christmas the worst part of John's death is Joe no longer pays her?"

Lyndon Johnson watched as Clark Gifford sat down across from him in the bar. "So what news do you have for me?"

"I've gotten the funds you wanted for Duvalier in Haiti. I don't know what good it'll do when rumor is Onassis is planning to help him build a resort there similar to Las Vegas. It is a prime place for Onassis to set up his shipping industry and make tons of money in cargos to and from Vietnam."

"You tend to your business and I'll tend to mine." Johnson snapped. "My spies say there is a cooling of sorts where Onassis is concerned and he may pull out of funding that deal."

"Your sources are probably spies for Duvalier and they would make sure you're duped for the monies. Sometimes you're green for a democrat." Clark opened his pack of cigarettes and tapped one on the edge of the desk.

"Don't waste your time lighting that, old boy, you won't be staying long." Johnson returned to the pile of papers on his desk.

Being the last to arrive, Barbara and Marilyn sat around the campfire surrounded by good looking men. Bill sat close to Marilyn and watched her as she roasted her marsh mellow to perfection.

Bobby and Jack had been staring at the fire in silence. They all looked up as the pilot walked up with a lean man following closely along the path.

"Hi Bobby, Derek here said you were on the island and that I could tag along with him." Frank held out his hand to Bobby but stopped when he saw Jack.

"Holy Mother of God," Frank swooned and fainted on the sand.

Mary Meyer left her hotel with the feeling someone was following her. She turned abruptly to catch them watching her but no one seemed suspicious. *How long are you going to keep this up you cold-hearted bitch? With you everything is personal isn't it?*

Mary continued along the avenue, stepping into Macy's department store to shake them.

Laughing to herself, Mary got off the elevator at the women's department and strolled to the evening dress section.

Ethel was thumbing through the gloves watching for Mary. As Mary came up to stand beside her, Ethel turned and offered her hand. "It's nice to meet you."

"I wish I could say the same but I've just shaken my spy who could see us at any moment. Let's go into the dressing room where he won't be able to follow us."

They quickly grabbed a few gowns off a nearby rack and headed to the changing rooms.

"Jackie's never going to give this up." Mary took off her shoes and placed them near the dressing room door. Ethel had taken the room next to her.

"What are you saying?" Ethel asked as she leaned against the wall closest to Mary's.

"Think about it. I had an affair with John that lasted two years."

"I knew that."

"I also have wondered about certain actions that led up to the assassination."

"Like what?"

"All I can tell you right now is that I'm afraid for my life. I have to go; I'll be in touch." Mary left the dressing room leaving Ethel baffled by the conversation.

Howard Hunt waited for Fidel Castro in the bar outside of the compound. *I'm not looking forward to this meeting.*

Castro came in and sat across the rickety table from Hunt. "Well, what good news do you have for me, my friend?"

"The news is not good. Marita is being protected by the CIA and we can't get to her now."

"Kill the bitch and her guards. She must be punished for this betrayal." Castro slapped the table with a flat hand causing Howard to jump.

"It isn't that simple and she's not worth it."

"If I say she needs to die then that is what will happen. Who do you think you're talking too?"

"Fine, but you should think about this. They know she was your spy, they will be waiting for anyone who comes for her and they won't kill them. Once they've trapped your errand boy they will question him and torture him but he won't ever get close enough to Marita to kill her."

"We are smarter than the Americans. He will succeed." Castro leaned forward with a furrowed brow.

"I doubt that. But it's up to you."

"Onassis, don't you understand Marilyn Monroe could still be alive. I want to find out. If she's still alive it could well be that the man with her was John Kennedy, our hated enemy." Papa Doc stood on the sand facing Onassis as the sun bounced off the waves behind them.

"Really, what difference does it make to us after all this time?" Onassis shrugged.

"Are you as ignorant of the world as that?"

"Careful Duvalier, how you talk to me, we are just friends on the surface." Onassis took out a pack of cigarettes, toyed with the package and replaced it in his pocket, "You shouldn't worry about who someone may or may not be. What Joannides and I plan to do with the Americans, specifically the CIA, well, suffice it to say, it'll create confusion and doubt from all angles. Trust me. Wait and you will see."

Chapter 46

Frank woke up in a darkened room disoriented and confused. *Where the hell am I?* He stretched and sat up as a wave of dizziness forced him to grab for the wall.

"Don't try to stand up just yet." Marilyn was seated across from him in an armchair.

"What happened?"

"You fainted. It was the craziest thing I've ever seen. Men don't usually faint." Marilyn leaned forward and handed him a glass of water.

He sipped slowly and rested his head against the wall. She took the glass from him setting it on the nightstand.

"Was he real? Was that really John?" Frank asked, running his fingers through thinning hair.

"Before I tell you what or who you saw you have to answer a question." Marilyn moved to the bed and sat down on the edge facing him switching on the bedside lamp as she did so.

"I'll try."

"No tricks Frankie, I need an honest answer, we all do."

"No tricks. I'm really at your mercy am I not?" Frank put his hand in his lap and watched her through doubtful blue eyes.

"True, it would be so easy to say you had drowned off the coast of one of the Hawaiian islands. The world would mourn your passing but of course it would be so like you to try and show off."

"What's the question, Marilyn? I'm not going to tell anyone about this if that is what you're all wondering."

"Oh no, we're not worried about that. We know you won't. The big question is, are you a communist?"

Lee and Jackie walked along the trail to the lake with John-John and Caroline racing ahead. The children were happily picking berries and putting them in a basket that Caroline carried.

"When do you plan to move to New York?" Lee asked.

"Probably before Labor Day, why do you ask? Are you afraid you won't get to see the children anymore?"

"Of course I love them but that's not the reason. I'm more afraid that I won't ever see Ari. I knew there was trouble when he gave you that expensive bracelet on his yacht." Lee kicked at a pebble and watched it roll away from her.

"You got one too."

"Not like yours. No one got one like yours. Even Maria knew you were trouble." Lee kicked at another pebble as they continued down the path.

"Big deal it was a little more expensive. Why do you care? Your handsome prince gives you the world." Jackie had stopped walking forcing Lee to stop and face her.

"You really don't understand do you?" Lee bowed her head for a moment and cleared her throat, "This is the one guy that would have truly made me happy and you don't care anything about him except for his huge pile of money."

"I thought it was all in fun, Lee. We've always played these games." Jackie watched her sister.

"Not this time, Jacks, it was much more than that to me." Lee stared into her sister's eyes. "This one hurts."

Jackie laughed, "Really Lee, you can be so dramatic. Go back to your prince and be happy with him."

"It's not funny, and besides you don't realize he's using you to get in nice and respectable with the American elite."

"I'm using him for far more than that, and I doubt even my name could give him what he wants from Bobby, the shipping docks or anything else in this country."

Johnson sat at his desk as Clark came in and sat down. "So what are you up to now, Lyndon?"

"I'm getting ready to send six hundred troops over to Vietnam."

"Why? We're not at war." Clark wrinkled his forehead in confusion.

"No, but we are involved in this conflict and I'm going to make sure the public sees the forward movement on how we'll stand up and defend against the common enemy." Johnson smiled across the desk at Clark.

"But they aren't our enemy."

"Not yet, but it's my business to make certain they will be."

"You've got to be kidding me." Frank looked surprised, "Of course I'm not a communist. Even Hoover, who has made my life a living Hell, has turned up nothing. Not a single shred of evidence to prove that not I'm one hundred percent American; even if I'm changing my allegiance to the Republicans."

"What was Johnson trying to prove?" Marilyn stood up and walked over to the small table.

"He wanted to link my ties with Sam Giancana to Fidel Castro and possibly with Khrushchev."

"When did you convince him that you were not a communist?"

"When Frank Jr. was kidnapped the media made a circus out of that so Johnson decided to dig a little deeper into my personal files. He looked into why I was never in the military and found out I was 4F."

"I always thought you had paid to stay out. The media said you paid forty thousand dollars not to enlist. Then later I figured you felt guilty and decided to go on a U. S. O. tour to make up for it." Marilyn turned back to him and sat down in the chair.

"You of all people should know the mob runs the media and you can't believe everything written there. They only print what they want the public to think." Frank shook his head.

"But with your ties to them, why would they want to hurt you?"

"Honestly, I'd pissed off Giancana and he was making sure I knew my place."

"Makes sense."

"She is taking a long time with him. What do you think is going on?" Bill stabbed a coat hanger into the fire and stirred it irritably.

"They have an interesting way of talking to each other." Jack laughed, "It could be hours."

"I don't think I can stand that. She may need rescued." Bill stood up.

"Sit down. She can take care of herself. She's been doing it a long time."

"Yes, but now I want to take care of her. She shouldn't have to do anything on her own." Bill slowly sat back down but stared at Jack.

Barbara snorted back her laughter, "Does she even know you love her?"

"Oh, Lord no. I haven't been able to tell Norma that yet."

"Well, there's something she hasn't told you either." Barbara took another swig of her beer and laughed at her own joke.

Ari answered the phone on his yacht hoping it was Jackie.

"Hello darling," Ava purred, "I've got some bad news for you."

"What is it?" Ari sighed, and sat down.

"I can't get you those tapes you wanted, darling. I've tried but now Bobby is away and no one knows where or when he'll be back. He wasn't in the giving mood the last time we spoke."

"Hmmm. Don't worry about it. I take my losses in stride. He may have won this round but I'll win soon enough." Ari grinned at the prospect.

"Oh, darling, I didn't know this was a child's game or I never would have gotten involved." Ava sounded annoyed.

"Don't pout, I'll send you a nice consolation prize. I don't want a beautiful lady like you to feel slighted."

"It's so nice when one is appreciated. Ta-ta darling."

Chapter 47

Mary stood against the fence as Ethel walked up. She was feeding the monkeys through the chain link and didn't notice Ethel was there.

"Hi." Ethel startled her.

"Hey." Mary turned to her for a moment and then back to dividing the treats into the greedy hands of the little monkeys.

"Were you followed?" Mary dusted her hands off and turned away from the now squealing animals.

"No. You?"

"I'm fine. My tail doesn't seem too interested in really following me. He stopped at a coffee shop as I came into the zoo."

"Tell me what is going on." Ethel walked down the trail with her to the orangutans.

"My best guess is that I know some key things about Fidel Castro, much like Marilyn Monroe did. What do I have in common with her other than an unusually high IQ?"

"John?" Ethel asked uncertainly.

"Yes, you're a smart cookie, don't feel intimidated." Mary chuckled.

"Thanks, I'll try to keep that in mind."

"What else do we have in common?" Mary prodded.

"I'm not sure of anything else. You aren't part of the Hollywood set but you do know all about politics. You're ex-husband is CIA."

"You did your homework on me. I'm impressed, Mrs. Kennedy."

"Ethel, please call me Ethel."

"Great. Now what conclusion did you draw from your research?"

"Other than a long lasting affair with John, I'm at a loss." Ethel sighed, feeling intimidated.

"We both kept excellent notes on political goings on. However, I don't believe I'm being followed as a political threat; nor, as possibly having communist ties; but because, put simply, I'm a woman in the same social class as our deceased president."

"Then who?" Ethel paused and looked at Mary.

Marilyn and Frank stepped out of the house and moved toward the campfire where the others still sat. "There's going to be a lot of political talk. Do you want Derek to fly you back now?"

Frank smirked, "And miss this? Are you kidding me?"

"I wouldn't want to leave either."

They walked down the path and stopped in front of the others. "He's okay." Marilyn chuckled and sat down in the sand next to Bill's chair. He immediately reached down and stroked her shoulder.

Marilyn glanced up at him in momentary confusion. The tender expression on his face told the full story. "I think I want to go for a walk, Bill. Are you coming?"

He stood up and followed her without a word as Barbara made an excuse to leave the men alone.

"So Frank, I bet that was the shock of your life." Jack handed him a beer.

"Never had one larger, even when Frankie was kidnapped," Frank chugged the beer and made a face, "I can't drink this stuff. Do you have anything else?"

"No. Are you hungry?" Bobby had gotten up and lifted a tin foil wrapped fish out of the coals along with a baked potato and placed them on a plate.

"Thanks." Frank took the offered plate and began opening the foil, "Tell me the whole story while I eat."

Papa Doc stood waiting on Maria Callas to finish her practice session for her upcoming tour of New York. As her pianist left the room, he approached her.

"I find myself enchanted by your rich voice, Maria." Papa Doc bowed over her hand and kissed the air above it.

"Thank you. What a pleasant surprise to see you here." Maria rubbed a hand across the back of her neck as the hair stood up on it, grabbed her bag off of a folding chair, and headed out of the practice room.

"I was wondering about the young woman who accompanied you in the "Diamonds" number."

"Norma?"

"Yes. I was hoping you had an address for her so that I could send her a bouquet of flowers. She is an unusually beautiful woman."

Maria laughed, "You men are all alike, aren't you?"

Papa Doc smiled back, "We know beauty when we see it. So do you know where I can find her?"

"I wish I could help you but she didn't leave me a forwarding address. The last place I knew she was staying was at the Ritz in Paris."

Bill walked beside Marilyn as the surf danced around their ankles. The moon had risen high enough for them to see the ground before them. Marilyn stretched her arms wide and took a deep cleansing breath.

"I could live here forever. Free from the worries of the world including politics." Marilyn kicked at the water.

Bill smiled as she enjoyed the moment, not answering or interrupting her fun. They walked along in companionable silence until the little airstrip came into view.

"Barbara made a strange comment." Bill began as they spotted her plane.

"Really? What did she say?" Marilyn turned to face him as she walked backward against the surf.

"She said you had a secret. Would you ever like to share it with me?" Bill grabbed her arm as she tilted toward the water. Marilyn smiled at him and put her free hand around his waist to steady herself.

"Why would she say I have a secret? I don't know what she's talking about." Marilyn stepped away from him.

"I'd say that you do but you don't trust me enough to share your secret. Haven't you realized by now how I feel about you Norma?" Bill stepped closer to her as their eyes locked.

"Bill, I haven't thought about you in that way. I mean I haven't dated anyone in over a year."

"No, you haven't dated, but you pretended to be married to me and I think that even Khrushchev was fooled. Maybe I don't want a pretend marriage to you, Norma maybe I want it to be a real one." Bill leaned closer to her lips and encircled her waist with his arms, "Don't you know? I love you."

Kenny listened intently to Lady Bird rattle on about drapes and china while he busied himself with notes. As she got finished with her story, Kenny frowned in disappointment.

"So Mrs. Johnson, is there anything else you wanted to tell me?"

"No, I don't think so. You're such a nice young man to listen to my domestic issues."

"It's my pleasure, ma'am."

Lady Bird got up to leave him, but stopped as she placed her glove on her hand, "Oh yes, there is one thing I wanted to ask you. Lyndon is no longer afraid of Onassis. Do you know why?"

Hoover lit a cigarette, satisfied with what he had learned from Jim about Mary Meyer. He scrawled some notes on a legal pad. *Mary Meyer - divorced, no children. Last known lover of JFK. Lives on the Potomac River. May know vital government secrets.*

"Jack, I'm so glad you're not dead." Frank shook Jack's hand before he began the meal Bobby had handed him.

"It's good to see you too." Jack laughed at him.

Frank ate as silence descended upon the thoughtful group.

"Now Frank, you know our secrets." Bobby leaned back against a log and stretched his legs toward the dying fire.

"I won't tell a soul what I know."

Marilyn leaned away from Bill, "This is too sudden for me. I've not had a chance to go from 'friends' to 'lovers' in my mind. I need a moment to think."

Bill dropped his arms from around her waist and took a step back, "I understand. Forgive me for being inconsiderate."

Marilyn laughed lightly, "You're always a gentleman, Bill. That isn't what I meant. Not really."

"What then?" Bill placed his hands behind his back and watched her in the moonlight.

"I want it all, you know. I've thought about this a great deal these past few years. I want a husband who will never leave me, a home that is secure and stable, and hopefully a few of my own children." Marilyn swept the sand with her big toe.

"I can give you all that and more. I desire to give you the home and family but also travel and adventure. I have thought about you constantly from the first moment I met you. Could you see your way to at least going out with me one evening?"

Chapter 48

"Okay Frank, now that you know our secrets it's time for you to spill some of yours. What do you know about Giancana's involvement with Castro and Onassis?" Bobby moved to get a little more comfortable against the log.

"I don't know much. I've totally distanced myself from Giancana and his goons since he messed me over on my gaming license."

"Understandable, I've always known you to be an honest man when you've decided to talk. So let's keep up the honesty here. What do you know about Maheu?"

"Robert Maheu is in deep with Onassis. Maheu came into the club a few months ago and sat with Johnny Roselli and Jimmy Fratianno. I couldn't hear what they were saying but it was something about a pay-off. Maheu handed them both an envelope, they slipped them quickly into their pockets but I saw them."

"What is Maheu doing in your club showing pay-offs where you can see him? Is it a warning to you?" Jack sat forward and put his hands closer to the coals.

"I'm not sure what he was doing there but he did want me to notice his little exchange. I'm not into any of the mob scene especially after what happened to my son."

"It was an obvious attempt to show you something. When I get back to DC I'll send Latimer and Stansel to hunt down Roselli and find out what he's been up too."

Jackie sat sipping her coffee in her favorite café when Papa Doc suddenly appeared at her little bistro table. Surprised Jackie looked up at his smiling face.

"Hello, Jacqueline. What a surprise to see you here." Papa Doc extended his hand to her. When she raised hers, he lifted it to his lips and kissed it.

"Hello, Mr. Duvalier, are you here on business?" Jackie took her hand back and placed it in her lap.

"Yes, as a matter of fact I am. I'm just passing some time until my meeting. May I join you?" Papa Doc seated himself in the chair opposite Jackie before she answered.

"Of course," Jackie wrinkled her brow at the intrusion but smiled at him.

"What would you recommend here?" Papa Doc held up the menu and placed it in her hands as he silently dropped a small capsule into her coffee cup.

"Are you wanting a snack?" Jackie asked as she looked over the menu at him.

"Yes, something lite," he smiled at her as he sat back in his chair.

"The croissant is nice." Jackie closed the menu and handed it back to him.

"Thanks, I'll go place my order." Papa Doc got up in time to see her lift the drugged coffee to her lips.

As everyone returned to the campfire the talk focused on the adventures Marilyn and Barbara and what they went through to get there. Frank and Derek were checking the plane for his return to Hawaii.

Marilyn leaned closer to Bobby, "And then Sam said Johnson is sending thousands of advisers into South Vietnam to train them in American military tactics."

"He's already planning to make this a full scale war. He's getting his people into position. Why?"

"Johnson also has been increasing his covert operations over in Vietnam and Sam knows all about it." Marilyn pulled her sweater closer around her.

"What the hell?" Jack suddenly stood up, "That should never happen. How can he do this?"

Bobby answered, "That's why you were removed. Johnson must have realized the power this would give him. He's more about power than wealth. I bet he's working with Onassis to ship his guns over to Vietnam to arm them."

"He's been investigated for money laundering, government misappropriation of funds, and bribery. I wouldn't put it past that son-of-a-bitch to line his own pockets." Jack sat back down, "What does Frank Sinatra have to do with this? Why did he see the pay-off with Maheu?"

"Jack, we need to talk while we're alone."

"Okay, about what?"

Bobby sat on the edge of the bed and took off a shoe. He held it for a second as he looked at his brother. "I need you to lay low for a while. There is nothing you can do right now to push who was behind the assassination. We're pretty much convinced that Sam Giancana, Roselli, and the rest of those thugs are working with Castro."

"But we can't prove it, Bob. You need someone to do that and I can. You know how I hate sitting around doing nothing."

"I do know, but you'll only get in the way. I'll take you back to DC and we'll have Kenny put you up for a while. He lives alone and outside the city. It's perfect."

"What will I do with myself? How can I just sit around all day and night and do nothing?" Jack leaned against the door frame with his arms crossed.

"I don't know, take up a new hobby or catch up on your reading of James Bond books. Just promise me you'll stay out of trouble."

Aristotle lay back on his chaise lounge on the deck of the Christina with George Joannides sipping champagne and soaking up the beauty around him. It was a gorgeous day and there were even more gorgeous women lounging topless enjoying his ogling eyes.

Ari smiled at George, "Now to talk a little business."

George tore his gaze away from the women and looked at Aristotle, "What do you want to discuss?"

"I need to create a little diversion in the CIA. Nosenko isn't talking, that is correct, is it not?"

"No, he's said all he's going to say and he's no threat."

"Nosenko is a moot point right now. I need to keep him from being believed even if he does decide to talk."

"What do you suggest? It sounds like you have a plan." George sipped his drink and watched Ari, "You always know where you are going before you suggest a 'talk'."

Aristotle snorted his laughter, "Of course, a shrewd man always knows his next move. Now I need you to help me with a defection."

"Now who is defecting?" George sat up straighter,

Ari had his full attention.

"I don't want him interrogated or harassed. I need him to defect cleanly or my plan won't work."

"How can I manage that on my own? I'm a double agent not a miracle worker."

"Jim Angleton will help you. I need my golden coin removed from Russia." Ari lifted his sunglasses off of his face and stared directly into George's eyes. "You know who I mean, right?"

"Anatoly Golitsin?"

Marilyn and Barbara had just landed on the small private airstrip outside of DC and taxied into the hanger. Barbara had invited Marilyn to stay with her for a day or two until Bobby got Jack settled in with Kenny.

"Is this your place?" Marilyn asked as she stood up to get out of the little plane.

"Yep," Barbara placed her clipboard in the log holder, "Come on and I'll show you around."

The women left the hanger and walked toward a large house with a white fence surrounding a manicured yard.

"I'm impressed." Marilyn shielded her eyes to get a better look as the sun began to set behind them.

"Don't be. It belonged to my parents. It's been in the family for generations so I can't take much credit. I live here alone now."

"No beaus?"

"No, you're the only one who has men falling at her feet." Barbara laughed as she walked onto the wide porch and unlocked the front door.

"I used to, but not that much now." Marilyn sighed.

"What about Bill? He seems to be completely gone over you."

"He won't be once I tell him the truth. He still doesn't know who I am."

"Honey, you have to tell him, unless you don't want to see where this romance of his might take you."

Marilyn didn't answer as they made their way into the house.

"Do you want to go out with him?" Barbara stopped with one foot on the staircase, "Honey, you need to pick up your life at some point, you can't keep hiding behind a bevy of Kennedy children. What do you want from life?"

Chapter 49

Papa Doc returned to the little bistro table and smiled at Jackie as he sat down his coffee and snack.

"You look a little ill, are you all right?" he asked as he poured sugar into his cup.

"Fine, I'm just feeling a bit strange."

"Tell me, did you enjoy being the first lady?"

"Mostly, but I didn't like Jack seeing so many women I knew."

"That would be hard." Papa Doc acknowledged smiling encouragement. "Who was he seeing that upset you?"

"Mary Meyer was the most recent. That little bitch was my friend."

Papa Doc tsk-tsked and shook his head. "What do you think would have happened if he had lived?"

"Nothing, Joe would have kept paying me to stay with him and I would have stayed, for a while at least." Jackie slapped a hand over her mouth as her eyes widened.

"What do you mean by 'at least'?"

"I want more. I always want more." Jackie was appalled at the brutal honesty she was displaying with him.

"More money?" he smiled sweetly, "Who would have more money than the Kennedy clan?"

"Ari, of course, he is the wealthiest man in the world." Jackie sipped her coffee and relaxed, "I don't know why I'm telling you all of this."

"Perhaps you know I'll understand." Papa Doc leaned forward and patted her hand. "I do have one question that perhaps you won't mind answering for me."

Jackie's eyes were dilated and she was pale but she nodded.

"Where is Jack Kennedy now?"

June 20, 1964

"Bobby thank God you have finally called." Ethel sounded panicked.

"What's wrong honey?" Bobby asked from the airplane phone.

"It's Teddy, his plane went down."

"Holy Mother of God is he alive? Please say he's still alive." Bobby tapped his foot.

"He's still alive but it's not good. He broke his back. The pilot and one of his aides are both dead."

Bobby sighed in relief, "I'll be home in a few hours. We'll go see him soon."

"I've already been and he's doing all right. Pat called Jackie and she refuses to come."

Kenny opened the door, "You're really here." The two men exchanged hugs as Jack dropped his duffle bag on the floor in the entry hall. "I can't believe it's you."

"I get that a lot. It's how Bobby reacted." Jack smiled and ran a hand through his hair.

"Where is Bobby?"

"Teddy was in a plane crash, don't you watch the news?"

"Not lately, I've been too busy spying on Johnson." Kenny led the way down the hall into the living area. "Is he going to be all right?"

"Yes," Jack looked around, "Nice place you have here."

"Thanks, it's really hard to get property on the Potomac but I love it here. I've got steaks grilling. Are you hungry?"

Mary Meyer stood frowning in her bedroom doorway. *Who's been here? Has the bitch had someone break into my house?* There wasn't any evidence that there had been a stranger in her house but she knew. There was a faint smell of a man's cologne lingering in the room.

Mary put her purse on the bed and dumped out its contents. A small diary fell out, she picked it up and tapped it against the palm of her hand. *I bet you were looking for this, but I'll never leave it where you can find it.*

Jackie sat with a fixed gaze staring at Papa Doc, "I don't know. He may be dead but I doubt that. I just don't know what to believe."

"Why do you think he may be alive?"

"I'm sure it really was Jack that called me on Thanksgiving. Everyone thinks I'm crazy that it's just because the events of the assassination were so horrific but I know his voice. He knew things that a prank caller wouldn't have known."

"So you think it was your husband who called you?"

"Yes," Jackie swallowed and ran her tongue over lips that were suddenly very dry.

"I noticed you seemed distracted during Maria's performance. Why?"

"I could have sworn he was dancing on stage."

"With Marilyn Monroe?"

"No, she's dead but he was dancing. It had to be him."

Bobby and Ethel walked into Teddy's private hospital room in West Springfield, Mass. Teddy was flat on the bed, while Joan held his hand. The entire family had gathered in the waiting area down the hall. Ethel and Joan left the room to allow the brothers a few minutes alone.

"Teddy, I'm sorry I took so long to get here. How are you?"

"Great. I'll be running in no time." Teddy smiled but it didn't reach his eyes.

"What happened?"

"Bad weather had us socked in. What I don't understand is why we were cleared for a landing when we should have been re-routed."

"I'll make certain there is a full investigation into that. Are you suggesting this was a plot?"

"I don't know but it seems like it could be with the death threats we've all been getting."

"Were there any indications you were going down?" Bobby shook his head in confusion.

"Just a sharp nose dive, the pilot said he couldn't understand why and we went down in the orchard."

Roselli stood talking to another thug as Latimer and Stansel snuck up on them. Roselli turned as Stansel tapped him on the shoulder.

"Mr. Roselli, a moment of your time," Stansel briefly flashed his badge as Roselli grimaced.

"What is this about? I've got business I need to attend to." Roselli stared at the ground.

"Right now, this business is more important. Either you answer here or we take you to headquarters." Stansel held firm as Latimer flanked Roselli.

"I see. You're going to play tough. Fine, but I doubt I can be of much help." Roselli looked at Stansel.

"What can you tell me of your involvement with Robert Maheu and 'The Weasel'?"

"I know them, so what? It ain't a crime to know people is it?" Roselli took out his pocket knife and began cleaning his fingernails with it.

"No, it's not a crime but we're sure that what you do for Maheu is. Why did he give you an envelope in Vegas? Hadn't you already been paid?" Latimer asked trying to throw him off guard.

"Yeah, we'd been paid but this was a bonus, see."

"Bonus? For what? A job well done or to keep your mouth shut about something?" Latimer reached out and took the knife forcing Roselli to look at him.

"Both - you stupid pig. What's it to you?"

"We were talking to Fratianno and he says you did the dirty work." Latimer began using Roselli's knife to clean his own nails.

"That's a lie. I don't have that kind of aim." Roselli smacked his hand over his mouth as his eyes grew wide.

Chapter 50

The stretch limo was now familiar to Jenkins as he stepped off the curb and opened the door. "I see that you've decided we meet in style."

Johnson smiled and puffed on his cigarette, blowing smoke rings towards Jenkins.

"Since you appreciate my style and class let's get right to business. Things need to move over there. We need to make sure this pigeon is able to take flight soon."

"Well, all the key players are in place. You only have to create an incident to get the ball rolling. What you need is a Hail Mary play." Jenkins straightened his tie and grabbed a can of soda out of the mini bar at his elbow.

"Give the go ahead for the radar blip. We need to justify this conflict into war by mid-August if not before. The plan is to make it look like the north is heating up."

"Anything for you, Mr. President, I just need a few days to get it lined out."

"Jenkins, you're a good man and you'll be amply rewarded for your efforts to your country."

"I don't need a reward. I'm just doing my job."

"Status, boy, every man needs it."

Ethel sat with her arms crossed in the back seat with Bobby as the driver took them toward home. Bobby sighed and tried to figure out what was wrong with her.

"Honey, please tell me what I've done wrong this time." Bobby tried to put his arm around her but she moved so close to the door he thought she might fall out.

"We didn't stay long, I said all the right things and..."

"Said all the right things? Is that what you think Robert Francis Kennedy!" Ethel stared at him in astonishment.

"What? Honey what did I say?" Bobby looked at a true loss.

"You said that you didn't blame Jackie for her reluctance to come see Teddy." Ethel shook her head.

"Well she does have the children to worry about..."

Ethel cut him off again, "Oh, of course she does but we don't have any children and can't make other arrangements for them to be watched while we visit your poor paralyzed brother in the hospital."

"Ethel, please be reasonable she just lost her husband." Bobby pleaded.

"No, she didn't. Jack died months ago and she needs to start understanding there is more to life than her perception of

Camelot and public opinion. Is she still a part of this family or isn't she?"

Barbara and Marilyn had enjoyed a couple of weeks relaxing and getting caught up on everything.

"So," Marilyn leaned forward and grabbed the last slice of pizza off the pan, "Howard enjoys living there and all of the glamorous people he sees, from a distance."

"Like who?"

"He has seen most of the Hollywood set as well as all of the Prince and Princess' around the world. He told me one story that was really interesting about Jackie Kennedy."

"Do tell, don't you hold back a single word." Barbara grabbed her beer bottle and took a chug.

Marilyn laughed, "Eager, I like that about you. So Howard told me while he found Jackie to be a beautiful woman he knew she would never find him equally appealing."

"Why would he think that? He's handsome in a freak of nature kind of way." Barbara snickered as she downed another drink.

"She likes them raw like animals."

"What?"

"Howard said she loves it rough and he could hear her and Ari one night on the balcony. He was curious and walked out of the secret passage way into the little vines. He looked up and saw them. They were both completely naked and his body was like those pictures of a Greek god. Howard wasn't able to look away. He was drawn to the cut Greek but also the way her porcelain skin glowed in the moonlight. He had never seen anything like it."

"Well, honey I think I need some of those special brownies I baked to help me get over that little image." Barbara began to stand up but Marilyn shook her head.

"I'm not finished, it's what she said to him that left Howard baffled."

"What?" Barbara sat back down and leaned in close to Marilyn.

"She told Ari she wasn't sorry, not one bit and she would have him for hers before long. She also said she would be damned if any other woman got to have John."

"When did all of this happen?"

"Sometime in the summer of 1962."

Bobby strode into J Edgar Hoover's office and sat down. Hoover looked up from the file he was writing in and laid the pen down on the desk.

"What can I do for you?"

"Whether we like the president or not is of little consequence at the moment. We need your boys to beef up the security to protect him. What happened to my brother can't be allowed to happen again."

"I'll get some of my best boys on it. We'll start training the best of the best to be body guards. What else?"

"Thanks, Hoover. I wanted to update you on the Soviet Union crisis."

"I'm listening. What do you have that I haven't already gleaned?" Hoover picked up the pen and tapped it on the file folder.

"Castro is behind the dissidents, he stands to gain control of the Soviet Union through the two new men that will be 'elected' after the premier is taken down."

"Of course I already knew that much." Hoover stopped tapping the pen as he looked at Bobby.

"Yes, well that is rumored to happen before the end of this year."

"I see. What does this have to do with the secret service and my branch?"

"Security needs to be beefed up world-wide. Onassis has Johnson under his thumb, while Castro is working the Soviet angle. We just need to protect our own."

"I'm with you."

Jack sat on the bench after Kenny had gone in to work and stared at the river. He drummed his hands on the wooden seat and stood up, moving into the house. He took a nice long shower and dressed in the most modern suit he could come up with. Taking a tie from Kenny's rack he fastened it with practiced ease around his neck and closed the front door behind him.

Hailing a cab, Jack barked an address and settled in for the ride. *Bobby is going to kill me.*

Papa Doc listened to the report with a growing frown on his face, "No sightings, no pictures and no media to prove what you say you saw. I'm sorry but we're at a dead end."

"You checked all of the media from all over the world?" Papa Doc demanded.

"Yes, we did. Our team is very thorough and we wouldn't dare come back empty handed if it were not true. The only thing we could find is this photograph taken at the funeral of JFK." The young man slid the picture across the heavy oak table to Papa Doc.

"Who are these people?"

"This is Ethel Kennedy and some of her of children with an unnamed nanny holding the baby."

"What good does this do me? Her face isn't even visible through the veil and her arm."

"It's all we've got."

Chapter 51

Jack strolled along the sidewalk in front of Jackie's new home and watched for any signs of life within. He had been patrolling the house, trying to look like a tourist for well over two hours.

He finally rounded the corner and spied a small café. *Well she apparently isn't home and my feet are killing me.* Jack went in, ordered a cup of coffee and sat down at a window seat. He watched the passers-by and sipped his coffee with his feet in the chair in front of him.

Jackie walked in on the arm of some of her oldest friends. She was smiling and talking, radiant in the afternoon sunshine.

Jack watched her sit down at a large table and after several moments, he got up, turned to the door and left, shoulders hunched down and head hanging. *I can't do it to her.* A few tears slipped down his cheek as he walked away from view of the window and hailed a cab.

"Ethel?"

"Yes, it's me. Who is this?" Ethel leaned into the receiver while she balanced the baby on her hip.

"Mary. Listen, I know I shouldn't call you at home but I'm sure I know who is following me now and why."

"I can get Bobby to look into it if you want me too. I'm sure he can help you. Who..."

"No, he can't help he's too close. I can't tell you who right now but I'd like to meet you soon so we can talk."

"Okay," Ethel began but the line had gone dead. Ethel stood for a moment and frowned at the buzzing phone before she replaced it into the crook.

Jim Angleton watched as George Joannides approached him with a file folder under his arm.

"What's this all about Mr. Joannides?"

"I have an assignment for you. We seem to have a mole in the bureau and I know you can help us clean it out." George handed the folder to Jim, "I'll be in touch."

Mary Meyer got off the bus and headed toward home. She watched the windows in the storefronts as she walked slowly down the sidewalk, her movements deliberate and suspicious. *Are you following me now? Why are you making my life so miserable?*

Rounding the corner to her street she noticed a man standing against the railing to the steps leading up to her little brownstone.

Mary stopped in her tracks, frozen in place as her mind raced, *Oh God, please help me.*

The man sensed her approach and looked up to see her standing still watching him. "Mary," it was barely a whisper but she ran to him and threw her arms around him, raining kisses all over his face. Finally their lips met and she sighed, leaning further into him.

A passer-by whistled loudly, "Get a room won't you? Some of us have children out here."

"Sorry!" Mary took the man by the hand and led him up the remaining steps and into the house.

Jackie frowned as Bobby stormed around the living room of her home. She sat watching him, in her favorite position with her feet tucked under her and a blanket tucked around them.

"How could you?" Bobby stopped and kneeled in front of her.

"I know Bob, I can be a real bitch sometimes," she put her hand on his cheek. "It wasn't that big of a deal now was it?"

"The entire family thought so. Teddy can't understand it. What am I supposed to tell them all?"

"Tell them that I just can't face all of you good looking men who remind me so much of John. I'm seeing my shrink and he's helping me come to terms with this but it's been exhausting." Jackie allowed a single tear to roll down her cheek.

"They'll understand, but you must make an effort to go see him. He's hurting and it would cheer him up to see you."

"I'll try but I can't promise anything. I'm so confused right now. I thought I spotted John in the coffee shop the other day. I've had nightmares since then." Jackie placed the handkerchief up to her nose and wiped with a delicate little swipe.

"You know that's impossible." Bobby smiled and patted her hand, *Jack I'm going to kill you.*

Marilyn opened the front door to find a florist standing there with a huge bouquet of roses.

"Ms. Norma Baker?"

"Yes."

"Sign here." He handed her a little clipboard and set the roses on the porch. "Have a nice day." He took the receipt and bounced off the steps hurrying to his truck.

"What's going on?" Barbara stepped onto the porch where Marilyn was leaning down picking up the gorgeous vase containing the peach flowers.

"It looks like someone sent these to me. Oh, how exciting. I haven't had flowers in years." Marilyn carried them in the house poking through them for the card.

"Oh, I bet those are from Bill Walton. That man is crazy about you."

Marilyn opened the tiny envelope and read the card. She handed it to Barbara with a puzzled expression on her face, "I don't think so."

President Johnson listened to the report given by the sonar man as it came through. His briefs about the attack in the North Vietnam waters were now being broadcast from the USS Maddox and would soon include another war ship, the USS Turner Joy. These skirmishes would soon be all he needed to pressure Congress into war.

Johnson smiled at this well laid plan. He picked up the phone, dialed and waited.

"Onassis? Johnson. I've good news for you. Our plan will be in place before the end of the week. Yes, the first of the little battles has taken place."

"Then I will ready my ships to help transport weapons. We were beginning to think you weren't going to hold up your end of the deal."

"It's well on its way to war. I'll say a speech later in the week telling the American people that we've been attacked and have a right to defend ourselves. It will do the trick." "My ships will be ready in the next few days. We stand to make a lot of money on this one, Johnson." Onassis hung up as Lyndon smiled.

Kenny searched his apartment but found no sign of Jack. "Shit!" he stormed to the living room and grabbed up the telephone.

Kenny dialed Bobby's home number but it just rang. Finally the housekeeper answered and informed him they were at the hospital visiting Teddy.

"What now?" Kenny fixed himself a drink and stationed himself in the living room to wait.

Marilyn took the card back from Barbara and reread it:

My darling, I've searched the world over to find you. You've been well worth it. Meet me tonight in front of the Washington Monument. I'll see you at 9:00.

"There is no way you're going to meet whoever this is. It may be an innocent romance or it could be dangerous. Maybe someone has figured out you're alive. Perhaps Giancana saw you in Barcelona." Barbara opened a beer and plopped down on the sofa.

"How would anyone have this address except for Bill?" Marilyn sat down across from her on the coffee table, "Let's think this through."

"I am thinking it through. What if there is a bug in that bouquet?" Barbara started to stand up but Marilyn held up her hand.

"No way there's a bug. Why would anyone do that? They want to see me not hear me. Try and calm yourself. We need to consider this from all angles."

"Okay, what do you suggest?"

"Who would want a meeting with me? It's not a 'date' it's more of a meeting. So, there's Sam Giancana, Papa Doc if he's still tracking me down and Bobby."

"Not Bobby. Oh, don't forget Bill there's always Bill." Barbara ticked him off on her finger.

"And Bill," Marilyn grinned, "we can rule him out. He'd ask in a gentlemanly fashion for a date. So, it's one of the other two or Sinatra."

"It doesn't make sense, and they're all dangerous." Barbara swept past Marilyn and reached for the phone, "I'm calling Bobby."

Chapter 52

<u>August 4, 1964</u>

Johnson sat behind his desk in the Oval Office and addressed the nation via television and radio. He was solemn and firm, "…air action is now in execution against gunboats and certain supporting facilities in North Vietnam which have been used in these hostile operations."

Cameras flashed in his face as he continued his speech explaining the necessity of this action, "The determination of all Americans to carry out our full commitment to the people and to the government of South Vietnam will be redoubled by this outrage. Yet our response, for the present, will be limited and fitting. We Americans know, although others appear to forget, the risks of spreading conflict. We still seek no wider war."

Johnson looked squarely into the cameras, "...firmness in the right is indispensable today for peace; that firmness will always be measured."

Lady Bird rushed to his side as soon as the broadcast was over and hugged him. "Great speech Lyndon, but why did you tell the Soviets we didn't want to pursue war after Hanoi?"

Papa Doc stood on the dock waiting for the Christina to pull up. As Ari disembarked the yacht, Papa Doc tied off the rope.

"What are you doing here?" Papa Doc asked, "It's not often you come to Haiti unannounced."

"I'm on my way to gather my ships. I just wanted to refuel and be gone again." Onassis headed down the pier, "Oh, one thing though, you put a voo-doo curse on the wrong Kennedy. Are you sure that was Bobby's hair?"

"He'll get his don't you worry about it." Papa Doc was offended, "I never make a mistake."

"Well, if you want my money and investors you need to make it happen." Onassis stopped and stared at the voo doo priest.

"Money is always what I need. It'll make me happy." Papa Doc started to walk but Onassis didn't move.

"Millions do not always add up to what a man needs out of life." Onassis shook his head, "No sometimes, status is more important."

"You mean a certain grieving ice queen in America could gain you status if the right Kennedy were dead, don't you? Tell me, Aristotle, do you really think she's going to bring that to you? They hate you over there."

"True, but they love her. She will bring me into her circles and I'll be accepted."

"I guess you can always ride the chaos so you'll come out on top. That's what I do." Papa Doc stepped off the end of the pier and prepared to leave Ari, "Oh, and one more thing my friend, you were right about Norma. I have satisfied myself. She's not Marilyn Monroe. Besides, I've got other more important things to chase after."

"Bobby said he will take care of it. You are to go and meet this mystery person and he will have agents all over it." Barbara sounded dubious. "I don't like it. I'm going with you."

"There is no need for you to come too. You've done so much for me all ready. I'll be fine. I just need to make sure I have a cab here in plenty of time to get me there."

"I insist on taking you. No more arguing. So do we want steak for lunch or fish?"

Jack came into the house to find Kenny sleeping on the couch. He headed up the stairs. He was trying to be quiet but one of them creaked and Kenny came awake.

"Where the hell have you been? Bobby is going to kill us both." Kenny jumped to his feet and stormed over to the stair case as Jack descended.

"I went to see an old friend." Jack smiled and shrugged his shoulders.

"Judging by the way you smell, like left over perfume and chocolate, I'm going to say it was a woman." Kenny smacked the newel post with a palm.

"Not just any woman, my friend, but one who was delighted to see me."

"You couldn't just let me hire you a hooker? I mean at least a whore wouldn't recognize you and potentially blow the lid off this entire secret." Kenny grabbed a bottle off the bar and poured himself a stiff drink.

"No, it was Mary. She wants me back. She says we can start a new life together. I need a life. Don't you understand that?"

Kenny sighed, "Yes, I can understand that you need a life. I can even understand a woman agreeing to be with you but what I don't understand, at all, is why it had to be someone from your past. Why risk it?"

"There's no risk. Mary hasn't told anyone anything up to now, so why would she ever say anything?"

"This Mary wouldn't happen to be Mary Meyer would it?" Kenny wrinkled his brow, downed his drink and slumped onto the nearest chair. "Jack you're an idiot."

Bobby checked in with Bill Walton just before seven that evening. "So, you'll be there with Marilyn as well as several other top agents in the field, right?"

"Right. I'll guard her with my life." Bill closed the door to his office and locked it up. "I'm going to go change into my running shoes and make one last sweep of the area where we're meeting. Is Barbara still going to bring her?"

"Yes, she is. That means she'll be protected and watched every moment. Don't worry, it's probably just some love sick sap she met in her travels." Bobby had started walking down the hall with Bill at his side.

"A love sick sap with excellent spy capabilities. How did he find her?"

"That is what we need to find out. Don't worry, you've got this thing covered." Bobby smacked him on the back, "You're a love sick sap too, aren't you?"

"The most powerful men in the world can wreak havoc with each other, but a damsel in distress turns the complicated business mind to mush." Jackie puffed her cigarette and watched her children play on the lawn.

Lee thought about her statement for a moment, "Jacks? What have you done?"

Marilyn and Barbara walked around the monument just as the lights began coming on around it as dusk set in. The night was clear but dark.

Several touristy looking people stood around admiring the view and milling around. Most of them began to drift away toward the park as the night grew darker.

Barbara recognized the secret service men as soon as they casually strolled into view. They were all wearing dark pants and short sleeved shirts with ties. She grinned to see they were trying to fit in with the tourists but they failed to her trained eye.

"I hope that whoever you're meeting doesn't catch on to our protection." Barbara nodded her head in the general direction they were standing.

"Relax a little, I'm fine." Marilyn scoffed at her.

Four men in full costume were walking around looking for a place to set up for an impromptu performance. Marilyn and Barbara watched them and tried to figure out what they were made up for.

"Look at the beautiful ladies." One of the men called to his friends, "Just what we need; a couple of volunteers."

Barbara shook her head, "No thank you."

Marilyn grinned and walked closer, "What kind of help do you fellows need?"

"We need one of you to stand here and the other one to stand over there," he pointed to the spots, "all you have to do is stand there."

"Come on Barbara we can do that. How long do you need us for?"

"Just a couple of minutes; while we go get our gear," he nodded as two of the men headed away while the women stood in place.

"I don't see what this can hurt." Barbara conceded.

Bill Walton and the agents were in place surrounding the monument in several areas. Bill was going to remain closest to the ladies as the rest of the men spread out around the area a few feet away.

Marilyn spotted Bill out of the corner of her eye and smiled an acknowledgement. So far everything was quiet and no one had approached her.

"Maybe Romeo isn't going to show up." Marilyn called to Barbara.

"I think he will. He's just trying to see if you'll wait on him." Barbara glanced at her watch, "It's only a few minutes after."

"Could one of you please come and help me carry this?" One of the costumed men came toward the women.

Marilyn smiled at Barbara, "You go. I'll stay here for my Romeo."

Barbara went into the darkness with a secret agent trailing far behind her.

The three costumed men were hanging around setting up little props that looked worthless to Marilyn. Bill idled across the walk toward her. "Watch carefully. I don't trust this."

Marilyn nodded as he kept walking. After a couple of minutes, the fourth man came back without Barbara.

"Norma?" he asked.

"Yes?" Marilyn's eyes widened in surprise and the beginnings of terror.

"Barbara says to tell you that she's not feeling very well and she'll wait for you in the car."

Bill heard this and walked back toward Marilyn just as the three costumed men leapt into action. One grabbed Marilyn around the legs, the other around the neck and they took off running while the third man stayed behind to see if anyone would follow suit.

Bill ran toward Marilyn as the agents swarmed around the third man.

Marilyn struggled as she was choked and carried to a large empty cargo van and thrown in the back through the wide open double doors. As the two men jumped in after her, Bill caught the back of a door and hopped up onto the bumper.

"GO! You idiot! We've got her." One of the thugs called up to the driver while trying to push Bill down. The other thug watched the struggle for a split second and let go of Marilyn. The van started moving as the smaller thug tried in vain to shut the back doors.

Marilyn opened the sliding side door and tried to jump free but one of the men grabbed the back of her dress and jerked her back in as the dress ripped down the shoulder seam.

"Now look what you've done!" Marilyn swung at him with an empty fist as she scanned the inside of the van for a weapon. She found the tire jack and pried it loose from its mount as the driver sped up. The van had left the parking lot and was bouncing along a bricked street.

Barbara, who had been dumped by the side of the road, stood up yelling, "Help!"

The agents rushed up on the scene while the fourth man, in cuffs, was being held in a cruiser.

Marilyn swung the tire jack at the back of the driver's head. He saw it coming in the rearview mirror and jerked to the left swerving the van as well. Everyone in the back jerked and swayed for a moment giving Bill time to regain his footing.

"Get that away from the crazy bitch before she kills us all," the driver yelled just as Bill made it into the van.

Marilyn lunged to grab the steering wheel while Bill fought the two men in the back. The van bumped across the curb and onto the sidewalk as the driver tried to land an upper cut to her jaw.

The agents on the street were running in hot pursuit of the swerving van. They were just gaining on it when suddenly it bumped off the curb, throwing Bill into Marilyn.

The thugs quickly jerked the doors closed and the van sped off, leaving the agents standing breathless in the street.

"Holy Shit! Mr. Kennedy is going to kill us!"

THE END

From The Authors

We had a lot of fun creating this alternate history of not only Marilyn Monroe, but also of John F Kennedy. We hope you enjoyed reading it.

Brightest Dawn, book three in the trilogy, is now available for purchase.

Look for exciting new titles as we continue to bring light and life to infamous people in history.

The prelude to the What She Knew trilogy will be out soon.

We would love to hear from you! To post a review, simply go to our Amazon book page. If you would like to stay in touch with us, you can go to the following link and sign up for our newsletter.

www.whatsheknew.wixsite.com/kandtproductions.com

Authors Page

K. R. Hughes is a native of Amarillo, TX. She has a degree in English, helps with literacy programs and tutors' college students. Hughes has two children, Justin and Kayti. Hughes also has two regency, historical novels, "Treasured Love" and "Lord Tristan's True Love," under her pen name Kymber Lee.

T. L. Burns is the foremost researcher and historical guru for the What She Knew Trilogy. Burns and husband Ken have two grown children, Kenny and Deven. Burns is a native of California. She has spent the majority of her adult life working with at-risk kids and adults.

Both authors currently reside in Las Vegas, NV where they write and encourage budding authors to follow their dreams. You can connect with them at any of the following social media groups:

www.facebook.com/HughesBurns

www.twitter.com/whatsheknewbook

www.whatsheknew.wixsite.com/kandtproductions.com

Cast of Historical Characters

Norma Baker (a.k.a. Marilyn Monroe)– sex goddess and movie star in the 1950's and 1960's.

Barbara Hadley – Norma's best friend and confidante.

John F Kennedy – president of the United States, nickname Jack. Married to **Jacqueline Bouvier Kennedy**.

Robert F Kennedy – brother to John F Kennedy and Attorney General for the United States, nickname Bobby. Married to **Ethel**.

Patricia Lawford Kennedy – sister to John and Robert Kennedy and married to **Peter Lawford,** movie star, one of the Rat Pack.

Joe Kennedy - father of John, Bobby, and Patricia; married to **Rose**.

Lee Radizwill - **Jacqueline Kennedy's** sister; married to **Prince Stasnislaw Radizwill** (aka Stas).

Teddy Kennedy - younger brother of John and Bobby.

Kenny O'Donnell - was an American political consultant who served as the special assistant and appointments secretary to U.S. President **John F. Kennedy**

Frank Sinatra – crooner, movie star and Rat Pack leader, political ally to John F. Kennedy.

Lee Harvey Oswald - was an American sniper who assassinated President John F. Kennedy on November 22, 1963.

Bill Walton – was the CIA operative who was the liaison to the Soviet Union.

Sam Giancana – mobster who wanted to further his career with anyone who paid well, also associated with Frank Sinatra and Jimmy Hoffa.

Fidel Castro – Dictator over Cuba, who had an alliance with Russia.

Nikita Sergeyevich Khrushchev - was a politician who led the Soviet Union during part of the Cold War. He served as First Secretary of the Communist Party of the Soviet Union from 1953 to 1964

Aristotle Onassis – Greek business tycoon. Bobby Kennedy was his arch enemy. He provided major business deals in the US through his shipping business – illegally.

François Duvalier, also known as **Papa Doc**, was the President of Haiti from 1957 to 1971

Mary Meyer – Her ex-husband is **Cord Meyer**. He works for the CIA in the 'dirty tricks' dept. She's a long-time lover of John F Kennedy.

Lyndon B. Johnson - Vice President to John F. Kennedy and became the 36th president of the U.S. when Kennedy was assassinated. He is married to **Lady Bird**.

Walter Wilson Jenkins - was an American political figure and longtime top aide to U.S. President Lyndon B. Johnson.

J. Edgar Hoover - the first Director of the Federal Bureau of Investigation (FBI) of the United States. Appointed director of the Bureau of Investigation—predecessor to the FBI in 1924.

Howard Hughes - an American business magnate, aviator, aerospace engineer, film maker and philanthropist. He was one of the wealthiest people in the world, and very eccentric.

Senator Margaret Chase Smith – A member of the Republican Party, she served as a U.S Representative (1940-1949) and a U.S. Senator (1949-1973) from Maine. A moderate Republican, she is perhaps best remembered for her 1950 speech, "Declaration of Conscience," in which she criticized the tactics of McCarthyism.

Smith was an unsuccessful candidate for the Republican nomination in the 1964 presidential election, but was the first woman to be placed in nomination for the presidency at a major party's convention.

www.ingramcontent.com/pod-product-compliance
Lightning Source LLC
Chambersburg PA
CBHW070219260626
47160CB00002B/605